PRAISE FOR TED DEKKER'S
BOOKS OF HISTORY CHRONICLES

"Young and old alike will enjoy this latest offering. Dekker fans will love this new story from the Circle universe and new readers will undoubtedly be sucked in to the greatness that is Ted Dekker. [*Chosen*] is a superb beginning to what is sure to be a fantastic series."

—Bookshelf Reviews

"Toss away all your expectations, because *Showdown* is one of the most original, most thoughtful, and most gripping reads I've been through in ages . . . Breaking all established story patterns or plot formulas, you'll find yourself repeatedly feeling that there's no way of predicting what will happen next . . . The pacing is dead-on, the flow is tight, and the epic story is down-right sneaky in how it unfolds. Dekker excels at crafting stories that are hard to put down, and *Showdown* is the hardest yet."

—Infuze Magazine

"As a producer of movies filled with incredible worlds and heroic characters, I have high standards for the fiction I read. Ted Dekker's novels deliver big with mind-blowing, plot-twisting page turners. Fair warning—this trilogy will draw you in at a breakneck pace and never let up. Cancel all plans before you start because you won't be able to stop once you enter *Black*."

—Ralph Winter, Producer of *X-Men*, *X2: X-Men United*, and *Planet of the Apes*

"[In *Showdown*] Dekker delivers his signature exploration of good and evil in the context of a genuine thriller that could further enlarge his already sizable audience."

—Publishers Weekly

You've heard about the critical raves,
but here's what readers are saying online about

The Books of History Chronicles

(Black, Red, White, Showdown, and *Saint)*

This trilogy is a MUST READ! Suspenseful, insightful, fast-paced, and certainly life-impacting. Ted Dekker is a master of bringing Truth close to home, in a way that causes us the readers to see and feel it in a fresh way.

D. (Pittsburgh, PA)

Whew, ok I've read all three books in the Circle Trilogy back to back and all I can say is man what a ride. **Ted Dekker has to be one of our generations great story tellers,** *this story of Thomas Hunter's fight to save mankind from a terrible virus intended to destroy the world is sure to become a Christian fiction classic much like Lewis's "Narnia" Series and Frank Perretti's "This Present Darkness."*

Todd (Mount Vernon, WA)

This was the first book by Ted Dekker that I've ever read. It was all I needed to be hooked for life! **Ted Dekker has a way with words and storytelling that not many authors have anymore.** *He draws you in and you have to make yourself stop for daily functions such as eating and occasional breathing!*

J. (South Carolina)

I cannot say enough good things about this book and series. It can change how you think. If a book can do that it is an amazing thing. I recommend it without reservation. The Circle Trilogy was my first Ted Dekker book, but it will not be the last.

Teresa (Parkersburg, WV)

Fascinating... worth the read.... I enjoyed the series so much I bought a second set as a gift even before I finished White.

Slwaldaias (Yerington, NV)

*This book, like Red, picks up where the last left off. The book is very quickly paced and makes it easy to fly through even if you're trying to slowly read it to take everything in. **By the time you're finished reading, you're just left speechless** with all the twists and turns in the plot. These three books are the best I've read in quite a while.*

Becky (Mentor, OH)

This is an incredible book! *Like all of Dekkers masterpieces, this plays with your emotions until your drained! By the end of a Dekker book, you are challenged to think, and on the brink of doing a million push-ups, (or crying depending on who you are.) Read this great book!*

Media Lover

*The writing is superb; fast paced, and always leaves the reader on the edge of the seat. **Ted Dekker is a writer of rare creativity and imagination.***

Michael

*As a consummate reader of fiction I can honestly say that this trilogy penned by Mr. Dekker is **perhaps the most absorbing and well executed tales I have ever read.***

Barb

These books were simply amazing. *I first heard about it after reading Thr3e. Once I picked it up, I could not set it down.*

J. (Seaside, CA)

*This guy is truly amazing. He's written straight novels, romance thrillers, psychological suspense, and now a fantasy thriller. He stretches and stretches, yet never becomes distorted, uneven, or sloppy. **I suspect that a generation from*** *now, Dekker's writings will be essential reading for those who wish to study spiritually motivated literature.*

Tommy (Federal Way, WA)

Absolutely a terrific trilogy! I got the first book, "Black" from the library, and when I finished it and realized it was a trilogy, ordered all three books the same day...next day! Incredible book full of drama, mystery, and beautiful love stories...both for people and God. You won't regret reading them...

June (Florida)

This may be one of my top 5 books of all time. The whole thing was engaging and outstanding. There was no lull anywhere. Each page and each chapter had interesting things happening. I've since read other's of Ted's including Red, White, Heaven's Wager, and Three. All awesome.

Sgun73 (Carmel, IN)

*This is the first of a trilogy - but don't be intimidated by the fact that you must read three books to journey through all of Dekker's tale. **This is an incredible fantasy, written with such a furious pace that it is hard to put down.** I was wise enough to not start any of the three books until I had all of them - unfortunately for my wife I did have all of them when I started reading them, and I just went from one to the next to the final one. Incredible!*

Zachary (Wake Forest, NC)

I am addicted to great story telling. Ted Dekker is now my main drug dealer. *I'm halfway through Red, the second book of the Circle Trilogy, and have now put Mr. Dekker in my pantheon with Robert Jordan, Stephen Lawhead, C. S. Lewis and Professor Tolkien. This guy writes literary heroine.*

Mike (Centreville, Alabama)

*I like books with lots of action. Dekker delivers. I love books that make you expand your inner universe. Dekker delivers. I enjoy books with great romance. Dekker delivers. I enjoy exotic locales. Dekker delivers. **I LOVE this book!** I highly recommend reading it! It totally keeps you on the edge of your seat from the very second you start until it leaves on a cliff-hanger for the next book in the series. You gotta get it!*

Trinedy

*The Circle Trilogy - Black, and the subsequent Red and White - is not the sort of book I usually read but I was persuaded to try it by a friend who had read it and loved it. I thought I would listen to just enough to be able to say I tried but couldn't get into it - **Boy was I wrong!***

Lynne (Montgomery, AL)

These books touched me more than any other books I have ever read. *I was reluctant to buy the books when I first heard what they were about. Finally said, "what the heck" and purchased them based on the great reviews. I am so happy I did. They are unlike any other books I have ever read and really cannot compare them to anything.*

Rich L (Pennsylvania)

Quite possibly this is one of the most incredible books ever written. *Definitely that I've read. Too bad I can't give it more than just five stars! I was so in awe of this story. I can't recall the last time I read a novel with such depth and magnitude.*

Sir iliad (Pennsylvania)

This is one book you can not put down. *I read all three books in three days. If you want a book to keep you occupied, then read this book.*

Cheri

*I just finished Red, and all I can say is "Wow"! This story just keeps getting better. Is Ted Dekker talented or what? Before I became a Chritian, I used to read secular suspense. **I must say this is better than anything I've read not only in Christian writing, but in fiction period.***

Nicholas (Salt Lake City, UT)

*WOW! **Ted Dekker continued to blow my socks off** in book two of the trilogy Black, Red, and White. The book held my interest, in fact it drew me to continually read to the point that I finished it way faster than most books that I have read(I think my wife was ready to put me out with the dog).*

William (Stouffville, Ontario, Canada)

*I am new to Ted Dekker: but I'll be getting further acquainted. The story kept me turning the pages; some of my guesses were prescient and others missed the mark. Captivating! **Where have I been as this author emerged in contemporary mystery fiction?** A great read!*

Lori (Lake Forest, CA)

*It is unbelievable how Ted can take your mind in so many directions at once and then tie all of it together and really put a spiritual meaning to the whole thing. **This is one of my favorite books of all time.***

Franklin (Warner Robins, GA)

*Ted Dekker did it again. **He got me wrapped around his fingers** (or writing I suppose). After months of wait I was not disappointed. This book is one of his best yet.*

Rafa S.

Dekker pulls out all the stops in this tale. I don't want to give too much away, but he really grabs you by the pants and doesn't let go! The blurbs are right, this ranks right up there with King and Koontz, not to be missed!

Matt (Mendocino, CA)

RENEGADE

teddekker.com

DEKKER FANTASY

BOOKS OF HISTORY CHRONICLES

THE LOST BOOKS
Chosen
Infidel
Renegade
Chaos

THE CIRCLE TRILOGY
Black
Red
White

THE PARADISE BOOKS
Showdown
Saint
Sinner (SEPTEMBER 2008)

Skin
House (with Frank Peretti)

DEKKER MYSTERY

Kiss (WITH ERIN HEALY—JANUARY 2009)
Blink of an Eye

MARTYR'S SONG SERIES

Heaven's Wager
When Heaven Weeps
Thunder of Heaven
The Martyr's Song

THE CALEB BOOKS
Blessed Child
A Man Called Blessed

DEKKER THRILLER

THR3E
Obsessed
Adam

RENEGADE

A LOST BOOK

TED DEKKER

THOMAS NELSON
Since 1798

NASHVILLE   DALLAS   MEXICO CITY   RIO DE JANEIRO   BEIJING

Published in Nashville, Tennessee, by Thomas Nelson. Thomas Nelson is a registered trademark of Thomas Nelson, Inc.

Published in association with Thomas Nelson and Creative Trust, Inc., 5141 Virginia Way, Suite 320, Brentwood, TN 37027.

Thomas Nelson, Inc. books may be purchased in bulk for educational, business, fund-raising, or sales promotional use. For information, please e-mail SpecialMarkets@ThomasNelson.com.

Cover Design by The DesignWorks Group, Inc.
Page Design by Casey Hooper
Map Design by Chris Ward

Library of Congress Cataloging-in-Publication Data [to come]
Dekker, Ted, 1962-
    Renegade / by Ted Dekker.
        p. cm. — (The lost books ; bk. 3)
    Summary: As Johnis, Silvie, Billos, and Darsal continue their quest for the four still missing Books of History, Billos makes a decision that has devastating consequences for himself and his companions, especially the devoted Darsal.
    ISBN 978-1-59554-371-4 (hardcover)
    [1. Fantasy. 2. Christian life--Fiction.] I. Title.
    PZ7.D3684Ren 2008
    [Fic]--dc22
                                2008000063

Printed in the United States of America
08 09 10 11 12 QW 6 5 4

beginnings

Our story begins in a world totally like our own, yet completely different. What once happened here in our own history seems to be repeating itself, thousands of years from now, some time beyond the year AD 4000.

But this time the future belongs to the young, to the warriors, to the lovers. To those who can follow hidden clues and find a great treasure, which will unlock the mysteries of life and wealth.

Thirteen years have passed since the lush, colored forests were turned to desert by Teeleh, the enemy of Elyon and the vilest of all creatures. Evil now rules the land and shows itself as a painful, scaly disease that covers the flesh of the Horde, who live in the desert.

The powerful green waters, once precious to Elyon, have vanished from the earth except in seven small forests surrounding seven small lakes. Those few who have chosen to follow the ways of Elyon are now called Forest Dwellers, and they bathe once daily in the powerful waters to cleanse their skin of the disease.

The number of their sworn enemy, the Horde, has grown, and the Forest Guard has been severely diminished by war, forcing Thomas, supreme commander, to lower the army's recruitment age to sixteen. One thousand young recruits have shown themselves worthy and now serve in the Forest Guard.

From among the thousand, four young fighters—Johnis, Silvie, Billos, and Darsal—were handpicked by Thomas to lead. Sent into the desert, they faced terrible danger and returned celebrated heroes.

Unbeknownst to Thomas and the Forest Dwellers, our heroes have also been chosen by the legendary white Roush, guardians of all that is good, for a greater mission, and they are forbidden to tell a soul.

Their quest is to find the seven original Books of History, which together hold the power to destroy humankind. They were given the one book in the Roush's possession and have recovered two more. They must now find the other four books before the Dark One finds them and unleashes their power to enslave humanity.

Although the full extent of the power contained in these sealed books is unknown, the four have discovered that touching them with blood creates a breach into what appears to be another reality. A breach they have been warned not to cross.

But Billos is not the kind to heed warnings. And his lust for the power contained in the books has overtaken all good sense.

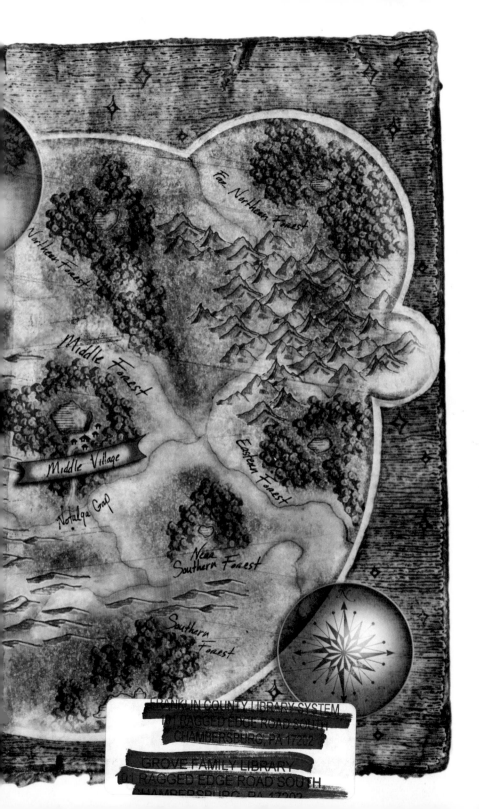

Far Northern Forest

Northern Forest

Middle Forest

Middle Village

Notalga Gap

Eastern Forest

Near
Southern Forest

Southern
Forest

one

Billos swung his leg over the stallion and dropped to the ground. The sun was blazing above the clearing, birds chirping in the trees. His horse snorted and lowered its head to feed on the grass.

He had to work fast. Knowing Johnis, the self-appointed leader would be coming with Darsal and Silvie soon. Johnis, this newly anointed major who could do no wrong. Not that he disagreed with the verdict—Johnis was a worthy leader of men. But the boy was holding something back, something about the books they'd each sworn to find.

Billos threw the saddlebag open, reached inside for the three books, and hurried to the boulder at the clearing's center. He didn't know what power came with having all seven books. Nor with opening a single book. In fact, he wasn't sure he had the courage to find out just yet.

What he did have was an insatiable need to feel the same surge of power that he'd felt the first time he'd touched one of the books with his blood.

He set the books on the stone, pulled out his knife, and ran the back of a trembling hand across the sweat that ran down his right cheek. The blue leather book on top stared up at him, beckoning, demanding, begging.

Touch me, Billos. Show me your blood, and I'll show you a new world.

He sliced his finger, wincing because he'd gone deeper than he'd meant to. Blood swelled. Dripped.

The sound of pounding hooves reached him.

Panicked that he might be discovered too early, he thrust his finger against the ancient leather cover. In the space of one quick breath the clearing vanished, replaced by the same darkness he'd seen before.

The power was still here! *There is more raw energy than I felt a week ago when I attempted the same with the others,* he thought. Or was it just the anticipation of what he intended next?

A distorted hole erupted before him, and from the darkness emerged the figure of the man dressed in black.

This could be Teeleh. Or the Dark Priest.

The man's long arm reached out for Billos, fingernails beckoning. A moan filled Billos's ears, so loud he thought the sound might be coming from his own throat, louder than the thumping of his heart, which crashed like an avalanche of boulders cut from the Natalga Gap.

Then the vortex opened to another place, not as dark. A six-foot hole in this world stood right in front of him, ringed in rippling blackness. A translucent barrier distorted what lay behind.

He reached out and touched the hole with his finger. Pushed it through. His finger went beyond the veil into a place that was warmer than the clearing.

Billos could feel his bones shaking, but his fear didn't dim his desire. He inched forward.

"Billos! Billos!"

Someone was calling his name.

He closed his eyes, took one last deep breath, and stepped past the barrier.

JOHNIS LED THE CHARGE TO THE CLEARING WITH SINKING hopes of finding Billos before it was too late.

"Billos!"

He saw the stallion through the trees. And past the stallion, Billos standing at the rock.

"Billos!"

Johnis broke from the trees and pulled up hard. Billos stood over the boulder, hand extended to one of the Books of History bound in leather. His finger was pressed against it. Blood pooled on the cover around a deep cut. The boy shook in his boots, like a goat hit by lightning.

Silvie and Darsal pulled their horses to a stop beside Johnis, eyes glued to the scene.

"Billos!" Johnis cried.

And then Billos disappeared, leaving behind a single flash of light that followed him into oblivion. And a bare boulder.

The birds were chirping; the horses were stamping; the breeze was blowing.

Billos and the books were simply gone.

Johnis, Silvie, and Darsal sat on their horses and stared, completely dumbstruck.

Silvie was the first to find her voice. "He's gone."

"They're gone," Johnis said.

two

For a long moment Darsal couldn't bring her mind to focus on what her eyes had just seen. One moment Billos had been standing over the books, finger extended, and the next he'd vanished in a flash of light.

And with him the books. But it wasn't the books that Darsal cared about now.

"Billos?"

Her voice sounded hollow in the empty clearing. She dropped to the ground and ran toward the rock, eyes scanning the trees for sight of him. Surely he hadn't actually disappeared into thin air!

"Billos! Answer me, for the sake of Elyon! This isn't funny!"

"He's gone," Johnis said. "I told you the books were dangerous. Now Billos has gone and done it, that fool!"

Darsal swung around and screamed at him, as much out of frustration at Billos as anger directed toward Johnis. "Shut up!"

Johnis swung down and approached, followed by Silvie. Both held her in a steady gaze. *The improbable events forced upon us over the last few weeks have changed us,* Darsal thought.

"Take it easy, Darsal," Johnis said. "Do I look like the enemy to you?"

"Take it easy? What do you suggest now, that I follow you to hell once again? Just head out into the desert and find Billos? He vanished before our eyes!"

"I'm not the enemy. Is that so difficult to understand? The books are gone because Billos is a fool—focus your anger at him, not me."

"Where did that imp go?" Silvie asked, blinking at the trees.

Darsal wanted to slap the girl, if for no other reason than she seemed so smug in her newfound confidence by Johnis's side. She had her man, this unlikely leader of warriors who didn't seem to know the meaning of the word *quit.* Not that Darsal resented Johnis or thought less of him than he deserved, but she felt that any attack on Billos was an attack on her.

If they knew what Billos had done for her all these years, they would understand. If Johnis was Silvie's man, then Billos was hers. In fact, much more so than these two who'd known each other less than a month. Billos was her savior, the only love she'd ever known, her life.

And now Billos was gone.

Darsal paced up to the boulder, ran her hand over the rough stone where the books had rested only a minute earlier. The surface was warm, by the books or by the sun she wasn't sure.

Johnis spit to one side. "What did I tell you? I should have taken them from him in the desert and kept them out of sight. Show Billos one ounce of trust and look what it's earned us!"

"You care more for books made of paper than you do for flesh and blood?" Darsal demanded.

"If they were just paper, Billos would still be standing here with a bloody finger on their covers."

He was right, of course. But that didn't change the fact that Billos *wasn't* standing here.

Johnis continued as if he'd read her thoughts. "I know you and Billos were . . . are . . . close. For that matter, I've risked my own life for him—"

"And he for you," she said.

"Yes, I suppose so. But you have to remember that the books must come first. We've all risked our necks for those three books, and we still have four to find."

Darsal paced, trying her best to remain calm. "For all you know, Billos has just taken the next step to *find* those blasted books! I can't believe you're taking this so lightly!"

Johnis started to nod.

"Were you the only one chosen, or was Billos also chosen?"

"All of us."

"Then quit pretending that the books are more important than he is!"

"Stop it!" Silvie cried.

Darsal grunted.

Here they stood, three new recruits to the Forest Guard—Silvie and Johnis just sixteen; Darsal seventeen—chosen for this mission that no amount of fighting or wit could accomplish.

Silvie was wearing a white cotton dress, an oddity for the fighter with short, tangled, blonde hair, who typically walked about in battle dress. She preferred to have knives strapped to her thighs.

Johnis had cleaned up as well, draped in a tunic as if he were as much a part of the council as the elder members. Even Darsal had attended the council meeting, from which all four had just come, dressed in a frock. Only Billos had turned up in battle dress.

Here they stood in a small clearing a ten-minute gallop beyond the outskirts of Middle Village, faced with a predicament that was more important than any could know—any of the hundred thousand or so Forest Dwellers who lived in the seven forests, now busying themselves with a meal or a dance or the sharpening of swords.

Or any of the millions of Horde who lived in the desert, cursing the forests and their dwellers, eating wheat cakes while they sipped wheat wine to ease the pain of their cracking skin.

Darsal walked around the stone, eyeing the bare surface. For as long as she'd known him, Billos had always been an impetuous little bulldog, getting them into as much trouble as he saved them from. She loved him; she was bound to him; she would die for him. But at the moment, she would just as soon strangle him.

His capture by the Horde had been beyond his control. But this time he'd run off without her. He'd abandoned her. She couldn't live with being abandoned by Billos. In fact, she wasn't sure she could live without him at all.

"You're right," she snapped, unable to stem her anger. "He may be a fool. But he's a fool whom I love." She rushed on, not eager to explain herself. "We have to find him! These books, this fate-of-the-world nonsense—yes, of course—but we have to find Billos!"

Johnis touched the stone and drew his hand back, rubbing his fingers. His eyes on her. "How do you search for someone who's left no tracks or scent?"

Silvie studied Darsal. "He did leave a scent. The smell of ambition—isn't that right, Darsal? He went into the books because of his thirst for power."

"And you wouldn't do the same to satisfy your thirst for revenge?"

They all knew Silvie's passion to avenge the death of her parents, who'd been killed by the Horde. She'd joined the Forest Guard as much to slay Scabs as save the forests.

"None of us is without blame," Johnis said. To Darsal: "You have my word, I'll track him to the ends of the desert if need be."

"Then you know there's only one way," she said.

Silvie frowned. "Say how?"

"Forbidden or not, dangerous as you might think, we have to match Billos's ambition or folly or whatever caused him to step past the barrier."

"Follow him?" Johnis said.

Darsal came closer, using her hands to express urgency. "You can't follow him into the desert, Johnis, because Billos didn't go into the desert. He went into the books! We have to find a book and follow him before it's too late."

"Too late for what?"

"Don't tell me you didn't see the Dark One the last time we touched the books."

"Teeleh," Silvie said, speaking about the leader of the Shataiki bats. "Or Alucard, his general."

"Or Witch," said Johnis. The Horde high priest. "But we can't just throw ourselves in because Billos did."

"Why not? You demanded that we follow you. And I doubt very much that Billos just disappeared from here to reappear with Teeleh or Witch. He's not in the desert; he's in another place altogether." She stomped for her horse, her mind clouded by her own need to find Billos. "We're wasting time!"

"Slow down," he snapped. "Even if we did agree to throw ourselves into the hole the way Billos did, we don't have a book. You can't just pluck one off the nearest 'original Books of History' tree."

Darsal spun back, started to tell him exactly what she thought of his cocky wit, then clamped her mouth and let her face grow red instead.

"He's right," Silvie said. "We have to continue the mission as if this hadn't happened. Find the books, find Billos."

"We can't just *continue* the mission!"

"Then what?"

"We have to drop everything and go after another book," Darsal cried.

"Exactly," Johnis said. "That *is* the mission."

"Now!"

"Yes, now. That's what we're doing. We're trying to get past all this emotion of yours so that we can calmly discuss the most logical next step."

"And that's what you did to find your mother?" Darsal demanded. "Fine, why don't we deceive a fighting group and get them slaughtered to find the next book. Is that the level of your commitment to Billos?"

"Enough!" Silvie stepped up, breaking their line of sight. "Both of you. You're both right: we have to find a book, and we have to do it now, but we can't run off into the desert without a plan. Think!"

She scowled at Darsal, then returned her attention to the center of the clearing. She walked around the rock.

"I can't believe they all just vanished like that. It's so . . ."

"Unnatural," Johnis said, joining her.

"Everything else we've experienced—the Roush, Teeleh, the Horde—it's all been the unseen becoming seen. But this . . ."

Johnis drew both hands through his dark hair. He was a good-looking boy with fine features and smooth skin, a poet and a writer before he'd been roped into serving with the Guard.

Billos, on the other hand, was covered in scars and had the muscle of two Johnises. A ruggedly handsome man. A true fighter who would take what was his and protect his own without so much talk.

For the moment Darsal paced and let Johnis and Silvie talk. A rustle in the trees drew her attention. She saw the fleeting white of a Roush, then the red eyes of a Shataiki bat that fled into the darkness beyond the branches.

"We see those two even though no one else can," Johnis said, looking up at the trees, "but we can't see what lies beyond the books."

"And who can see beyond?" Darsal demanded.

"Michal." Johnis nodded toward the west where Michal, one of the wise ones among the Roush, lived in the treetop village they'd visited a week earlier.

"Michal's the one who told us not to touch the books with blood," Darsal snapped.

Johnis faced her with a scowl. "You think he would lead us astray? If we go to him now?"

"There's someone else who knows even more about what is beyond what we can see." The idea came to Darsal only a moment before she spoke.

"Who?"

"Someone who may have actually gone where Billos is now."

She turned for her horse and had her foot in the stirrup before Johnis caught on.

"Thomas? That's rumor."

"And this talking won't amount to bird droppings," she snapped, swinging into her saddle.

Johnis hurried forward. "It's forbidden to tell anyone about the books! You have no idea what harm that will bring! You can't talk to Thomas about Billos!"

"No? Watch me."

Darsal kicked her mount and galloped into the forest.

three

Thomas of Hunter, or Thomas Hunter, as he would say if asked, was walking the southern path that skirted the lake next to the Thrall, explaining the ins and outs of fundamental forest living to Karas when the commotion on the opposite beach caught his attention. A lead horse chased by two others, tearing up the sand. Village houses crowded the beach behind the scene.

"Is that a game?" Karas asked, watching the beasts race around the lake's perimeter.

"It's three rascals who need their hides whipped," Thomas said. "Horses aren't permitted so near the water."

"Isn't that Darsal being chased?"

He looked closer and saw that she might be right. "You can see that from here? Never mind, of course you can. I forget how dramatic the change is at first."

Johnis had brought Karas, daughter of the Horde high priest, out of the desert with him. Her painful conversion from Scab to Forest Dweller had been her doing, when she'd washed herself in lake water and had watched her skin heal before her eyes.

Johnis had risked his own life for a Scab, and in so doing delivered much more to the forests than he had anticipated. The ten-year-old girl was a gold mine of information on the Horde's political and religious machinery, and Thomas intended to hear it all.

But at the moment his mind was on her humanity, her wit, her charm, not simply her use to them. *She speaks with the intelligence of a girl much older than ten,* he thought.

Before being cleansed by the lake water, her skin had been gray and cracked, her hair matted and dark, her eyes nearly white.

Now she looked across the lake with blue eyes that peered through soft bangs lifting on angel's breath. Her skin was newborn, flawless.

"So you know her?" Karas asked in a sweet voice.

"Who?"

"The one in trouble. Darsal."

He glanced up and saw that the riders behind—Johnis and Silvie, if he wasn't mistaken—were catching Darsal. Karas was right; there was trouble.

"She's from the Southern Forest. A victim of difficult circumstance. Why do you ask?"

The girl shrugged. "I think she's a pretty woman."

"No shortage of those. You've seen Rachelle, my wife. There's a looker."

"My mother, Grace, was pretty."

"Oh? Killed by the high priest . . ." He stopped and chided himself for mentioning her mother's death so casually. "I'm sorry—"

"Don't be." Karas kept her eyes fixed on the riders, who were now rounding the lake. "We've all faced a lot of death."

True indeed. "Darsal reminds you of your mother?"

"She could be her."

"Darsal, your mother? Then she would have had you when she was seven years old, because Darsal's only seventeen."

"Of course."

Thomas squatted next to the girl—this angel who'd come to them from the Horde.

Johnis was right; she was a gift from Elyon. Though Thomas wasn't ready to extend the same sentiment to the Horde warriors who swung mallets at his men's heads.

"Johnis's father, Ramos, insists that you should live with him, but my wife and I—"

"Your wife's a very intelligent woman," Karas said

"Yes. Yes, she is. And she joins me in extending an invitation for you to live with us if you'd like."

Karas shifted her eyes and stared into his. "We'll see. But you are very kind, Commander."

Thomas playfully brushed her chin with his forefinger. "Where'd you get such a bright mind?"

"My father isn't exactly an idiot. He's deceived."

The horses pounded closer. Clearly, this was no casual social call. Thomas stood and put his hand on the girl's shoulder. "Do you mind leaving me alone with this *trouble*, as you put it? You'll find Ciphus in the Thrall."

"I'd rather not."

He looked down at her. "No?"

"I'd rather see what this trouble is all about."

"I'm sure you would. And one day, when I make you a lieutenant, I'll let you settle matters like this." He couldn't help a gentle grin. "Though what could possibly be the problem now is beyond me. Maybe I should just let you deal with them."

"Okay." Karas made no move to leave.

Darsal raced in, pulled her horse to a rearing stop, slid from her saddle, and dropped to one knee. "Requesting an audience, sir!"

Her long, dark hair was pulled back and tied, baring the scar on her left cheek. If anything, the scar accentuated her cheek's firm lines and her soft lips. A fine woman, a fierce warrior, a passionate heart.

Thomas squeezed Karas's shoulder. "Leave us," he said.

She hesitated only a moment before turning and jogging down the beach toward the Thrall.

Johnis and Silvie jumped to the ground and hurried forward. But they seemed at a loss for words. This was Darsal's show.

"What is it this time?" Thomas demanded.

"We must lead an expedition into the desert immediately, sir," Darsal said, head still bowed. She looked up at Thomas. "Billos has gone missing, and we have reason to believe that he's—"

"What she means to say," Johnis interrupted, "is that we can't find Billos. She's in love with him. You understand how that goes. Her mind is totally—"

"Silence!" Thomas had chosen the four from a thousand fighters, and despite their rather unique accomplishments in these last weeks, they were erratic, untamed, impulsive, and in general a very high-maintenance lot. If not for the half-circle birthmark on Johnis's neck, which confirmed that Elyon had chosen the boy, Thomas thought he might reconsider his choice.

"What do you mean, Billos is lost? You've all just been found, for the love of Elyon!"

"Billos is a hothead," Johnis said. "It seems he's . . . well, we don't know that he's actually missing yet, do we?"

"No, we really don't," Silvie said, eyes holding Thomas's.

Darsal stood to her feet, staring, mind clearly spinning. Quiet for the moment.

"Well?" Thomas demanded. "Is Billos missing or isn't he?"

"He's missing all right," Darsal said.

"And is it true that you are in love with him?"

She breathed deeply through her nose. "Yes. So I would know if he's missing."

"How so?"

"Billos and I are . . . very close."

"What makes you think he's not just sleeping under some wood pile?"

Darsal hesitated. "Sir, is it true that you've been to a place beyond this world?"

Thomas felt his pulse surge. A dozen distant memories flooded his mind. It had been thirteen years since he'd dreamed of Earth, thanks to the Rhambutan fruit that kept him from having *any* dreams when he slept.

"Who told you this?"

"It's well-known."

Thomas dismissed them with a hand and turned away. "Don't believe everything you hear."

"You deny it then?"

"What does this have to do with Billos?"

"Billos—" Darsal started, but again Johnis interrupted.

"Billos was talking about your . . . dreams, whatever they were, before he went missing. Darsal seems to have linked the two. Please, we are wasting his time with this, Darsal."

"And why are you trying to shut her up?" Thomas asked.

"Am I?" Johnis shot Darsal a hard glance. "I wouldn't want to do that."

"You're obviously dancing around something that has you all bothered," Thomas said. "Less than a day has passed since you came out of the desert, nearly dead, and already you're running around like frantic little rodents, sniffing for trouble. Truth be told, I'm in no mood to play games at the moment. So . . . have no fear, Johnis, I won't push for the moment. But I will know everything; you do realize that."

Silvie looked at Johnis, who stood six inches taller than her and was broader across the shoulders. His otherwise boyish features made him appear only slightly less feminine than she. Johnis's weapon was his brain, not his brawn. Silvie, despite her petite frame and delicate features, was perhaps more brawny than he. Certainly the better fighter.

There is love between these two, Thomas thought. He should discourage two sixteen-year-old squad leaders from pursuing their love for each other, but something about Silvie and Johnis's attraction felt right to him.

Without offering any explanation, Thomas stripped off his shirt, loosed his boots, dropped his sword, and strode to the lake's edge. He dove into the cool water and let Elyon's healing power refresh his skin. "Bathe once a day to cleanse yourself of the disease," Elyon had told them. "Until I come to save you from evil in one fell swoop, as prophesied." Thomas had heard the words himself.

He rose from the lake, threw his head back, and filled his lungs with fresh air. He turned and drilled the three fighters on the beach with a stare.

"It wasn't long ago that I could breathe Elyon's water. Do you believe that?"

He walked out of the lake without bothering to wipe the water from his skin. "Do you?"

Johnis answered, "Yes."

Thomas snatched up his shirt. "And do you believe the rest of it? That the Roush once flew overhead, protecting us from the evil Shataiki? That Elyon lived among his own? That there was no disease?"

Silvie glanced up at the treetops to their left, then gave Thomas a look that seemed to ask if he'd seen it. *What?* Thomas had no clue, because the trees were empty.

"Of course, we believe," she said.

"That there are Books of History that contain a perfect record of all that has happened?"

"Yes."

"Then you're wiser than some who've lost faith in what they can't see."

"How does this lead us to Billos?" Darsal demanded.

"You asked if it was true that I've been to a different reality," Thomas said. "If you didn't believe in what can't be seen, I wouldn't want to waste my time answering. But since you do believe—and I'm assuming that includes you, Darsal—you'll find it easier to accept the fact that I have been to a place beyond this world, as you put it."

They stared at him, waiting for more explanation.

"In fact, there are millions of people who would swear to you that I'm asleep in a hotel in Bangkok at this very moment. That I live in the histories, two thousand years ago. They could show you photographs of me in bed, where I've been sleeping for the last thirteen years."

"Thirteen years?" Darsal said. "You look quite awake to me."

"I've only slept part of one night in that reality, dreaming of the last thirteen years here. They would tell you that you yourselves are just a dream."

He shrugged into his shirt. "You, on the other hand, might tell me that my dreams of Bangkok are just that, dreams I had while asleep here. Now ask me, which reality is real?"

"Which is real?" Johnis asked.

"Both," Thomas said. "The fact that none of us can see Bangkok doesn't mean it's not real any more than the fact that we can't see fuzzy white Roush in those trees means *they* aren't there."

Darsal's face lightened a shade. "So, you're saying that it's possible for someone to step beyond this world? That Billos could easily have vanished into this dream world of yours?"

"What have you been drinking? I'm sure you'll find Billos hiding behind a wood pile, sleeping off his ride through the desert." But Thomas could tell that none of them believed it.

"Please, you're not suggesting that Billos actually *vanished* into thin air," Thomas continued.

"No," Johnis said. "It was you who suggested it."

"I was talking about me, and then only about dreams."

"Either way, it sounds as preposterous as Billos vanishing. Not that he has, mind you."

"It does," Thomas said. "But my dreams were true; I can assure you of that. Do you know what they call Elyon in that reality?"

"Billos?" Darsal suggested.

Thomas ignored her. "God."

"So you're saying you won't help us," Darsal said. She was consumed with the notion that Billos had vanished.

And what if he has? Thomas thought. *What if Billos has somehow crossed the breach between worlds? Impossible, of course.* Rachelle would have a fit if she knew his thoughts.

"Absolutely not. I should put you in the brink for pushing such a fool's errand. Not even an idiot would suggest that I risk warriors to find a fighter who's been lost less than an hour. None of you are idiots, which leads me to believe you're hiding something from me."

All three looked at him with unwavering eyes, like deer before the flight.

"Now your silence confirms it," he snapped. "I'm your commander; tell me what's going on."

"It's nothing," Darsal said, pulling her eyes away.

"And you're lying," Thomas said.

"What she means is that it's nothing to anyone but us," Johnis said. "A very private, personal thing. We've taken a vow not to whisper a word about it to anyone, but you have my assurance that we will deal with it."

Interesting. They were hiding more than they could say without breaking their word. That Johnis had confessed this much rather than attempt to cover up further was at least noble.

All of this confirmed Thomas's suspicion that the four were up to something beyond him, beyond all of them. Why Elyon had chosen these four scrappers was still a mystery to him, but then again, why he himself had been transported from the streets of Denver to this land was a mystery as well. He, a street fighter who'd grown up in Malaysia, elevated into such a position between worlds.

He would treat them as he would any new leaders, but there was more at work here. In time he would know it all, assuming he lived until that time.

"I trust you to keep your loyalties straight," he said.

"Of course." Johnis and Silvie dipped their heads. Darsal stared at him, still lost in her own thoughts.

"Yes?" he demanded of her.

"What? Yes . . . yes, of course."

"Then take this very private, personal thing away from me. And for the sake of Elyon, prove yourselves worthy of the faith I've placed in each of you."

Johnis swung into his saddle. "We will, sir. Rename us the Three Worthy Ones if you wish. Nothing will—"

"Three? There are *four* of you."

"Of course, it's just that there are only three here, now. Four. The Four Worthy Ones."

Thomas didn't like the far-off look in Darsal's eyes, but he didn't want to push the matter further.

"A bit juvenile, don't you think, Johnis? Instead I'll give you a charge. I want the three of you to stay together until you find Billos. Consider yourselves each other's prisoners. Don't leave the village, and don't let the other two out of your sight. Am I clear?"

"Yes, sir," Johnis replied.

Silvie mounted. "Yes, sir."

Darsal was in her saddle, turning without responding.

"Darsal?"

"Hmm? Yes, yes. Of course."

four

The first thing Billos felt was the warmth. A heat that spread from his fingertips as they entered the hole in the air, up his arm as it passed the barrier. The burning sensation intensified as his face pressed into the translucent film of power.

It occurred to him that this hole might be nothing more than the mouth of death itself. That he could and should pull back. But the sound of hooves, thundering into the clearing behind him, pushed those thoughts from his mind.

He thrust his head through, and his body effortlessly followed. He was in.

Darkness. A surge of power ripped through his body, and for a moment all he could see were the stars that ignited behind his eyes.

The heat swelled. Pain sliced through his chest, his head, his nose. So intense now that he thought blood might be streaming from his eyes and ears.

Billos cried out and threw his hands to his head. Felt his mouth spread in a scream. But the only sound he could hear was a chuckle that echoed around him in the darkness.

He'd found death.

The stars behind his eyes began to move toward him. Past him. As if he were moving through them.

Without warning the stars became a blinding explosion of light that forced him to gasp.

This is it. This is it!

But then the light vanished, and Billos found himself standing in a room.

A white room.

A room filled with both terror and wonder at once.

five

"Now what?" Silvie asked, pacing the hand-hewn boards that had been strapped together to form the floor of Johnis's house. Johnis stood at the shuttered window, staring out with his hands on his hips, lost in thought.

Darsal sat on a stool by the table, sweating. It wasn't a hot day, but her face felt flush, and her hands were tingling. Sitting here after an hour of pointless discussion . . . she might as well be in shackles, locked in a cell.

The floorboards creaked loudly each time Silvie placed her weight on them. Evidently Johnis's father, Ramos of Middle, didn't have the time to fix his own house.

Darsal couldn't stand this a moment longer. "Will you please stop that?"

"Stop what?" Silvie asked.

"The boards are screaming bloody death. I'm trying to *think*!"

"Then think without being so sensitive," Silvie retorted. "I'm sorry that Billos was so selfish to leave you behind in his betrayal of us all, but you don't need to take it out on me."

In that moment Darsal wanted to reach out and slap Silvie's pretty little face. She, with her man standing pompous in the corner, loyal to the bone. But Billos was as loyal as Johnis, even if he did express that loyalty with more subtlety.

"He didn't *betray* us," Darsal snapped. "He's forcing the issue as any good leader would do."

"Forcing the issue by breaking his word," Johnis said, walking back from the window.

"And did you break your word to Thomas of Hunter in the desert this last week?"

Her accusation caught him flat-footed.

"Of course, you did. So watch what you say against Billos, both of you! As of yet he hasn't gotten anyone killed."

She stood and crossed to the same window Johnis had parked himself by. Outside the village bustled with people as the afternoon sun slipped farther into the western sky. The nightly celebration would soon sweep the beach. Song and dance and stew over blazing fires—with the Horde snatching life from them faster than they could make it, any excuse for a celebration of what remained was not only justified, but demanded.

But Darsal had no life left to celebrate. Not without Billos. He should have known better than to leave her in this fretful state. If and when she did catch up to him, she would wring his neck!

"We can't stay here," she said.

"We have to," said Johnis.

"We have to find another book."

"You talk as if it's a matter of going to market—just go out and select another book. And we can't undermine Thomas."

"You had no problem undermining him when it served your own—"

"And I was wrong!" he snapped. "We all know that now. I can't—I won't—do it again."

Darsal seethed. "We have to find another book and follow Billos. You know it's the only way!"

"For all we know Billos will pop out of thin air right here, in a few moments."

"We can't just stay here," Darsal repeated. "Elyon has given us an order. Our mission is to find the seven original books, four of which are still missing."

"All seven are missing, if you count the three with Billos," Silvie said.

Johnis sat down on the stool Darsal had vacated and crossed his arms. "We have to find the books, and we will. But we can't just run off and defy our commander, not again. Michal will come to us. Patience."

This newfound loyalty to Thomas of Hunter will prevent Johnis from being as inventive as he'd been when searching for the first book, or his own mother, Darsal thought. If Johnis had proven one characteristic beyond a shadow of doubt, it was his stubbornness.

But Darsal had no choice. They'd left her with none. She could wait here for Billos to magically appear, which wasn't a choice at all, or she could do what needed to be done without them. And she knew what needed to be done.

With each passing minute the conviction to follow Johnis concerned her less. Billos's betrayal stung more. And the urgency to join the only man she could ever love consumed her most. Johnis and Silvie had both betrayed their superiors. Maybe it was her turn. But fooling Johnis wouldn't be like falling off a rock.

"You asked us to follow you to the end of the earth," Darsal snapped. "And we did. You demanded we spare the Horde, and we did. Each time you were right. Now you say sit and wait. Are you right this time?"

He shifted his eyes away. "Would I have said it if I didn't think so? Based on what I know, yes, I think so. Silvie?"

Silvie shrugged. "It has to be right."

Darsal pushed herself from the wall and sighed. "You'd better be, Scrapper." She headed toward the hall. "But that doesn't mean I have to like it."

"None of us do," Johnis said. "Where are you going?"

"Please tell me waiting doesn't mean I have to hold my bladder too."

He regarded her for a moment, then nodded. "At the end of the hall. Silvie—"

"You're joking. I may be a little discouraged, but I'm not so depressed that I can't undress myself!"

Johnis blushed.

Darsal tromped down the hall, entered a small bathroom, and banged the door closed. "I'm not a child, Johnis!" she yelled.

She was moving already. With a flip of her wrist she unlatched the window, stuck her head out to check for prying eyes, and satisfied that she was in the clear, thrust herself headlong into the opening.

She coiled so that her legs followed her torso over the sill, landed on one shoulder with a soft *thud,* and rolled to her feet.

No sounds from the house, not that she could hear over her own pounding heart. She was free.

Six

The front of the house, where Johnis might be keeping an eye out, was to her right. So Darsal sprinted left between two other houses, then south toward the forest's edge.

Her horse. She needed the sword in its scabbard, the battle dress in its saddlebag, the water . . . dear Elyon, she couldn't forget the water!

No member of the Forest Guard wandered farther than a hundred paces from his horse—one of Thomas's standing rules in case of a sudden attack. They had tethered their horses to a feeding trough three houses south of Johnis's. No sign of pursuit. With any luck, Johnis and Silvie still didn't know she'd left them. But they would, sooner rather than later.

She grabbed a bridle from a rack next to the trough, swung

onto the saddled—always saddled—steed, and urged the beast through the gate. Several passersby gave her a casual glance, but she didn't care if they saw her go, as long as they didn't follow. That she had gone would be—maybe already was—obvious. Where she'd gone would be less so.

Darsal kicked the mount and galloped down the street, took a sharp left off the main road, and entered the forest.

A hundred thoughts crowded her mind, and only one, no matter how ludicrous it seemed, felt compelling. What was slow in coming through patience could be gotten much faster through force.

She had to make up for these last few hours of wasted time. Billos had gotten himself into terrible trouble, of that she was sure. The fact that he hadn't returned meant one of two things: Either he *couldn't* come back because he was dead, Elyon forbid, or hurt, or in some other way incapacitated. Or he didn't *want* to come back.

She moved fast, cutting back and forth every two hundred meters to slow the pursuit of even the best trackers. Not until she was a mile south and at least as far west of the village did she begin to call out for the Roush.

"Hunter!" The name of the one who'd led Silvie and Johnis to the Roush village a week earlier.

"Hunter!" She thought she heard a rustle, but no fuzzy, white, batlike creature flew in. "Hunter. Any Roush, I need you!"

The words felt stupid, not unlike those who cried out for

Elyon's salvation after a bloody battle. Save us, save us, O Elyon! And always Elyon seemed to maintain his silence.

Now she was yelling at the sky for a white creature that no one other than she, Johnis, and Silvie could see. And Billos, though Billos wasn't here to see.

"Hunter!"

"You're trying to wake the dead?"

Darsal pulled hard on the reins and spun back. A white Roush, roughly two feet in height, with wide wings and a furry, round body, perched on a branch, watching her without concern.

It had been a few days since Darsal had actually seen one of the creatures. And never before then. No one had seen the Roush since the Great Deception. Seeing a Roush now, so close, so real, still sent butterflies through her belly.

"You're alone," the Roush said.

"Are you Hunter?"

"One and the same. And you're Darsal, one of the chosen. Why are you alone?"

"Why shouldn't I be?"

"Because I was told that you were under strict orders not to leave the village."

Darsal realized her mistake then. The Roush knew what was happening, which meant that Johnis would soon know what was happening. There was no way she could make it to the Roush village without Johnis, Silvie, and even Thomas knowing exactly what she was up to.

She looked back through the trees. Still no sign of pursuit.

You're throwing yourself off a cliff, Darsal. How far will you go for him?

She answered herself immediately. *As far as Johnis would go to find what is precious to him.*

"Are there others around?" she asked. "Like you, I mean?"

"Roush? I can cover a flank by myself, thank you. But, yes, there are more."

"Where?"

"To the east, near the lake. Where you should be, I'm guessing. You humans always do manage to lose your way."

To the east, good.

"You're right; I should be bathing in the lake. But before I hurry back, I have a burning question."

"Then put it out."

"Put what out?"

"Your burning question. Douse it in lake water."

"I was hoping *you* could put it out. By answering it."

"Fine, fine. I'll do my best. I have been known to 'crack the wit' now and then." The Roush swept down and landed on the path, grinning at his own humor. "You do understand," the Roush said. "It's a play on words . . ."

"Yes, yes, of course. Crack the whip; crack the wit. Do you mind sitting closer, on the horse? Can you do that, or will the horse bolt?"

"No, not a problem." Hunter leapt up to the mount's rump. "You see. Not a problem; none at all."

"Hmm. The horse doesn't even know you're here?"

"Sure it does. And it could sleep like a chick with me perched on its head, for that matter. Roush are enemies of no one but Shataiki."

"Really? You could sit on its head? Show me."

Eager to demonstrate, Hunter flew around Darsal, landed with both claws between the horse's ears, and grinned. "Not bad balance, eh? I'm not scratching him, or he would bolt. Gentle as a leaf. Now, what is that question?"

Darsal wasn't sure how to go about capturing a Roush, but she'd convinced herself that she had no choice. Too much was at stake. Billos needed her.

She leaned forward as if to ask the question in a quieter voice, then shot her hands out and clamped them around the Roush's soft belly.

"What, no, that tickles! No, no!" Hunter began to cackle with laughter, loudly enough to wake the forest.

Now fully committed, Darsal tugged the animal toward her and was immediately rewarded with wings whacking at the air.

"No, no, you're killing me! I'm too ticklish!"

"Quiet!" Darsal tried to flip the bat creature around so that she could muzzle it, but its wide wings tangled with her arms, pulling her off balance. They both tumbled from the horse and landed in a heap.

Hunter squawked, alarmed. "What?"

She pounced on the creature, threw her hand over its snout,

41

and pulled it close. "Quiet! Be quiet. I won't hurt you, but I need you to be quiet!"

The Roush squirmed and almost broke free, forcing Darsal to clamp her arms tighter. "Stop it! You're going to get hurt. Settle down!"

Hunter settled. They were tangled on the ground, human and Roush: an odd sight, to be sure.

Darsal released its wet snout long enough to snatch a knife from her thigh and press it close to the Roush's neck.

"If you raise an alarm, I'll be forced to make my point. I'm sorry. I don't want to do this, but I need your help."

Hunter whimpered.

"We're going to get on my horse, and I'm going to have to restrain you with some rope. I won't hurt you, but I can't leave you here to turn me in."

Still no words from the talkative Hunter.

"You can speak now; just keep it down."

"Have you lost your sense?" the Roush demanded. "What are you doing?"

Darsal glanced at the trees. "You're going to help me find Teeleh."

Seven

Billos stepped back, half his mind on the frightful scene in this white room, half on the thought there might be a hole in the air behind him through which he could make a quick escape.

He felt behind him: nothing but empty space. A quick glance confirmed that the gateway had closed, stranding him in this small room, roughly ten paces per side.

No sign of the books.

He closed his hands to still a shiver and tried to make sense of the strange sight before him. The stench of fire filled his nostrils. Not wood smoke, but the kind of fire that came from burning rubber trees. Only there was no fire, not that he could see.

The room was white, square, with something that made him think of water on one wall. Perfectly smooth, dark water contained in large rectangles. Square "pools" of water that did not spill, even though they were on their side.

He stared at the water, distracted from the other wonders in this room. Six similar but much smaller square pools of water were fixed to the opposite wall in two rows of three.

Billos tore his eyes from the shiny surfaces and scanned the huge, fixed monster in the room's center. What appeared to be chairs or beds or wings of some kind surrounded a large rock.

A perfectly smooth white rock with dark eyes set around the crown. Or was it a giant white mushroom? Black roots ran from the white rock-mushroom into the wing-beds.

In some ways the monster looked like a spider with six legs jutting out of a round white body. Billos blinked at the thought. He touched the knife at his waist and took another step back.

Looking at the beast, he was sure that it was indeed a massive white spider, now sleeping, but sure to waken the moment it realized that prey had fallen into its gargantuan square web.

The flat pools were its drinking source, perhaps, which left Billos as food. He'd stepped out of the green forest into a spider's white trap! But the beast wasn't moving, not twitching, not breathing that he could see. Did spiders breathe? He didn't know.

The spider-beast had a tattoo stenciled under one of its eyes. Four letters: D-E-L-L.

A name?

Why would a spider have a word on its torso? Billos straightened. So then maybe it wasn't a spider at all.

He glanced behind his shoulder again, hoping for the gateway, but saw instead what appeared to be a white door.

Without stopping to consider where the door might lead, he rushed to it, grasped the silver knob, and twisted. But the handle refused to budge.

Whirling back he let out a slow, long breath. The DELL spider—if that's what it really was—hadn't moved. Now that he was starting to think a little more clearly, Billos was quite sure this beast wasn't a spider.

Since when did spiders have doors on their webs? Since when did spiders have square webs? Since when did spiders collect water in their webs?

When you enter a forbidden world created by the Books of History, that's when, you fool.

So then it *could* be a spider. But there seemed to be no immediate danger, and the courage that had brought him here in the first place began to return.

Think, Billos. Just calm down and think. First things first. You must find the way out.

He searched the walls for another door. None. He tried the silver knob again, all the while keeping one eye on DELL. But the handle refused to budge.

So he carefully edged over to the large square pool of water on the wall. Still no movement, no sign of immediate threat. Facing the shiny dark pool, Billos reached out and touched the water's surface with his index finger.

The water didn't yield. Only then did it occur to him that this wasn't water after all. He pressed the surface with his palm. This was a cool, hard surface, like perfectly formed black glass. The kind Thomas had taught them to make from sand.

Billos spun back, heart hammering. DELL still slept. Not a sound, not a breath of air, not the slightest movement.

What would happen if he touched the beast? He gripped his knife tighter. But his reason began to return, and once again it told him that this couldn't be a spider. Spiders could sense prey from a long way off. You didn't catch a spider taking a nap or looking the other way.

For a long time Billos considered his options, which seemed particularly limited to him at the moment. Then, reaching deep for the same boldness that had served him so well on many occasions (never mind that it had also nearly cost him his life on as many), he inched forward, reaching out his knife, and touched the very edge of one of the beast's legs.

Nothing.

Billos started to let the wind out of his lungs. But then nothing became something, because at that moment the beast named DELL opened one of its eyes.

Billos leapt back, crouched for what would come next. *It is okay*, he thought. He was bred for battle. Better to die fighting than from starvation in a spider's trap.

He would take the offensive and slaughter this beast where it crouched.

eight

She'd never imagined, much less planned, the kidnapping of a Roush before, and at first handling the creature unnerved Darsal. But really it wasn't so different from handling a small, furry human with wings.

Withdrawing a length of rope from the saddlebag, she quickly tied the creature to the pommel in front of her. To any Roush or Shataiki casually observing, she hoped it would appear that Hunter was just along for the ride.

"I'm sorry, but I'm going to have to bind your snout," she said, looping the rope over the Roush's mouth.

"What? You can't mean it! It's inhuman."

"*You're* not human. And, yes, it is a bit cruel, but I can't risk you making the kinds of sounds that might draw your friends. I'm committed now."

Hunter set his jaw and sat stoically as Darsal bound his jaw shut. It ruined the casual riding-partner look, but she had no choice.

She quickly dressed in her battle clothes that were in the saddle-bag. A leather skirt, protective leg and arm shields, a breastplate. Then she swung behind Hunter and galloped into the forest, toward the lake's north end, where she dipped out of the forest long enough to fill her water bags.

Johnis and Silvie would be searching by now, informing the Roush maybe, launching a search from the sky. But Darsal was headed into the northern half of Middle Forest, which was largely uninhabited.

Time was slipping, and Billos was . . . dead? Running? In chains? Being tortured this very moment, while Darsal, the one he'd risked his very life for, sat on a horse fretting over what consequences she might face for kidnapping a furry white animal?

Hunter rode smugly in front of her, warm back against her belly. Refusing to look at her, refusing to show the slightest concern.

"We're far enough from the village; I'm going to let you talk," Darsal said, stopping below a large nanka tree that hid the sky. "Nod your head if you swear not to give an alarm."

The winged creature squared its round shoulders and sat still as if he hadn't heard.

"You're refusing to help me find Billos, the man whom I love?"

Hunter turned his green eyes up and peered into Darsal's. He finally dipped his head.

"Yes, you're refusing to help? Or yes, you're agreeing not to sound an alarm?"

"Hmmm, humm . . ."

Darsal couldn't understand, so she slipped the loop off his mouth.

"Fine. Thank you for allowing me to swallow my own spittle."

A cloud of regret and sorrow suddenly settled over Darsal, and she had to lift her face to hide her stinging eyes.

"I won't raise an alarm," Hunter said. "But you know this is a mistake. No good can come of trying to find Teeleh."

"You're afraid of him?"

"I spit on his face. I detest the air he breathes; I vomit at his sight." Hunter had gone from settled to heavy breathing in three phrases. "If you hadn't abandoned your search for the books, I could see your going after that beast, but there's—"

"But I haven't abandoned the search! To find Billos I need a book. That's exactly what I'm doing: I'm going after a book."

The revelation made the Roush blink its round, green eyes. "On your own?"

"Never mind the questions; it's not your place to understand my logic. If anyone knows more about the books' whereabouts, it's the Shataiki, so—"

"What makes you say that?"

"If the Roush knew more about the books, Michal would've told us. According to Johnis, the Horde know nothing more. That leaves the Shataiki, who are obsessed with finding the books. If anyone knows more, it's them."

"You'd have to be both foolish and desperate to go after Teeleh. Besides, it's not Teeleh you want. If anyone does know more about the books—which I doubt, mind you, I sincerely doubt—it would be that other mangy one under him. Alucard."

"You're sure about that? Alucard?"

"Cut from the same rotting flesh."

Darsal's heart slammed. "Where can I find Alucard?" she asked, then swallowed.

"The Black Forest, naturally."

"It's gone! We—"

"Not that one. A forest two-days' ride north. There are seven such forests, all hidden to you humans. This one's hidden in a hole west of your Northern Forest. But I have to tell you, it's not a place you want to . . ."

Darsal kicked the horse and turned it north.

"So that's it, eh? You're just going to ignore my warning and head straight into trouble? Then why bother letting me speak, if nothing I say is more than noise to you?"

"Please, spare me the drama or I'll put the muzzle back on."

"Foolish, foolish, foolish prodigals."

"I don't have a clue what you mean."

"Humans who run off on their own and find disaster."

"I don't need to find disaster," Darsal said. "It's found me." She urged the horse into a trot. "Do I need to muzzle you?"

Hunter bounced in front of her, silent for a few beats. "No," he finally said in a heavy voice. "I suppose I'll have to come along to save your neck. But I do wish you would have let me kiss Teagan and Martin before leaving."

"Teagan and Martin? Who?"

"My two children. I have a terrible feeling they will be left fatherless."

IT TOOK THEM AN HOUR AT A FAST CLIP TO REACH THE FOR-est's northern border, where Darsal pulled up the horse and stared at the flat desert, stretching as far as the eye could see. Ominous, but she'd been through enough desert in the last few weeks to deal with any danger that came from the elements. Apart from the foreboding voices that kept flogging Darsal's thoughts, nothing threatened their progress.

Nothing, that is, until a horse stepped out from the trees behind them.

"Darsal?"

She spun her mount, forcing Hunter to frantically spread his wings to keep from falling. There on a brown mare that was ten times her size sat Karas, the little Horde girl who was no longer Horde.

Darsal was too stunned to speak.

"Well, well, well," Hunter crooned. "Well, well, indeed. Hello, little girl."

Karas showed no sign she'd seen or heard the Roush. But, of

course, only Billos, Johnis, Silvie, and Darsal had had their eyes opened.

"What are you doing here?" Darsal demanded. She scanned the tree line for others, but it appeared that this squat had come alone, unless she was being used as bait while they hid in the bushes. "Are you alone?"

"Yes," Karas said. "Except for the horse, that is. Do you count horses as companions?"

"People, you little fool, not horses."

Karas frowned. "You think I'm a fool?"

Darsal scanned the trees again, just to make sure there was no one else.

Eyes on Karas. "You're a fool for following me. What do you think you're doing out here by yourself?"

"Following you."

"Yes, following us," Hunter said.

"Just you remember our agreement," Darsal snapped at the Roush.

"What agreement?" Karas asked.

"Nothing. If you head back now, you'll be home before it gets dark. I suggest you get moving."

"I could take her," Hunter said. "She'd get lost on her own."

"Why would a fool who's followed this far turn back now?" the little girl on the huge horse said.

"Because following me into the desert would be even more foolish," Darsal snapped. "Because they're probably already screaming for you back at Middle. Because you have no reason to follow me in the first place!"

"Would I be here if I didn't have a reason?"

"Only if you really are a fool."

"She doesn't look like a fool to me," Hunter said.

"Shut up, Hunter," Darsal said.

"Hunter?" Karas blinked. "My name's Karas, and it's not polite to be so harsh."

Darsal set her jaw. "What reason do you have to follow me?"

Karas hesitated, then nudged her horse closer. "Does the name Grace mean anything to you?"

"I don't know, should it? I'm telling you, you'd better head back before—"

"She was my mother. My father, the high priest, killed her."

Darsal sat still. No matter how frustrated she was at the girl's presence, she didn't have the heart to tear into her the way she wanted to.

Karas continued. "She used to say that somewhere out there I had an auntie, because she had a younger sister—fifteen years younger—a long time ago. I think that I've found my mother's sister."

"Me?"

"You look like her twin."

"Don't be ridiculous. She had to be much older . . . She was a Scab."

"Weren't you listening? I said her sister was much younger. Thomas told me that when the Great Deception ruined the world thirteen years ago, families were broken up. The disease took most

TED DEKKER

of their memory. But I can swear you're mother's sister because you look like my mother. Except for the scar."

Darsal didn't know how to respond to such an absurd claim. "Is this possible?" she whispered, then prodded the Roush for an answer.

"Yes. Yes, of course it's possible," Hunter said.

"Yes," Karas said.

The forest's edge stood tall and silent. Darsal couldn't accept it, not after the years of suffering following her parents' deaths.

She calmed herself and let anger creep into her tone. "Either way, you can't just walk up to people and latch yourself on to them without knowing what's happening."

"Which is what?" Karas asked.

"Which is none of your business. This is crazy. It's going to be dark in an hour!"

"Then we'll build a fire," Karas said.

Hunter offered a soft chuckle.

"No. We will not. I will, not you, because you're not coming; it's out of the question!"

Karas seemed unfazed. "I insist. I don't know what you're up to, but it looks like you're headed out into the desert. I know the desert better than you."

"We know it well enough. You just escaped the desert, for Elyon's sake! Your insolence is infuriating!"

"We? You and I? So you're saying I can come?"

"Slip of the tongue. I certainly don't mean you."

"I can help you survive danger," Karas said.

"You're a ten-year-old squat!"

"I have more water."

"She has more water," Hunter said.

Indeed, having just been healed by the lake water, she seemed especially enamored with it. Two full bags rested over her saddle.

"Where are we going?" Karas asked.

"Nowhere." Darsal turned her mount, kicked its flanks, and trotted into the desert, begging reason to catch up to the foolish little girl.

"That's it, show her who's the boss," Hunter quipped.

"Quiet."

Taking a Roush to a Black Forest to find Alucard was one thing. Taking a young girl whom Johnis had risked his life to save—whom Thomas Hunter had taken an inordinate interest in—was madness.

The way Darsal now understood her situation was that she had a two-hour head start on Johnis, who would come after her as soon as Karas returned with the news that she'd headed north. But two hours were all she needed.

"We should head west first to avoid the Horde camping in the north."

Darsal spun in her saddle and saw that Karas followed ten feet behind, undeterred.

"She's right; the Horde is camped north," Hunter said.

"You can't come! Thomas will have my head!"

"I hope to help you keep your head, Big Sister," Karas said.

"And stop calling me that. You don't know it's true."

"I do know. I also overheard you talking to yourself about going to the Black Forest in search of Alucard, one of the legendary Shataiki that Witch often talked about. Don't worry, you'll grow to appreciate me."

"Why do you speak like that?" Darsal demanded in frustration.

"Like what?"

"Like you're a scholar rather than a child? I thought the Horde were stupid."

"Deceived, not stupid. And I'm not Horde anymore, or didn't you notice?"

Hunter sat grinning like a monkey. "Amazing," he muttered. "For all you know, Elyon has sent her to save your skinny neck."

"Don't be stupid."

"Keep telling yourself that, you might listen," the Roush said.

Darsal took one more minute to consider her options, which were either to return with the girl or press on in the hopes of saving Billos.

She'd escaped from Johnis's house thinking that life was hers to risk. Then she'd taken Hunter by force, and now Karas was in her care. The equation had changed. But her desperation to find Billos had not. And she'd already committed herself.

Their lives, all three of them, were on Billos's head, not hers.

Darsal humphed and galloped toward the sinking sun, followed closely by the little girl who claimed she was her niece and insisted on calling her "sister."

The world is coming apart at the seams, she thought. *First Billos, and now Karas. They are mad, all completely mad.*

nine

The spider named DELL stared at Billos with glowing, pupil-less red eyes. A whole circle of them ringed its head like a crown. They hadn't actually "opened" per se, but they had come to life and were peering at him.

Still, the beast did not move.

Billos had been in tight, life-threatening situations dozens of times, and if there was one thing that had been cut into his instincts, it was the importance of seizing the advantage. He had to move now, while he had the element of surprise. Surely the beast was as stunned as he; what else explained its inaction?

Billos feigned left, then darted to his right, knife still extended. His plan was simple: disable one leg, maybe two if he had the opportunity; leave his enemy vulnerable on one side, then keep to that side.

He thrust the knife into the thigh, twisted, and ripped backward. The skin tore, bled a white fluffy substance.

Feathers.

Billos jumped back, confused by the sight. The creature had not reacted. It hadn't even flinched.

He lowered the knife and stood up. So then, it wasn't a spider, not an ant, not a beast of any kind. This was a flower, or a bush, or . . . a tree maybe. Or a weapon of some kind. Maybe a fancy buggy.

And since the wall looked like the glass Thomas insisted came from his dreams, perhaps this object also came from his dreams.

For that matter, maybe Billos had stepped into Thomas's world.

He walked forward and tentatively touched Dell's leg, then decided that his first instinct had been correct. This was a chair or a bed, not a leg. Which meant he was supposed to sit or lie on it.

For the first time since he'd crossed into this strange and terrible place, Billos grinned. A daring, fascinated grin with just a little relief.

This didn't end his troubles, of course—he still had to find a way out before he starved to death. The books were nowhere to be seen, and he didn't have the slightest idea what the contraption did or how to work it, but at least he wasn't pinned under its hungry jaws.

"So, so, so, what do we have here?" he muttered. "Tell me what surprises you hold for me, DELL. Let's make friends."

Armed with his new conclusions, Billos slowly ran his hand

over the cut he'd made. A chair. Yes, of course, how foolish of him to think this contraption was a spider.

DELL was undoubtedly a horseless buggy. Six reclining seats and a spokeless wheel in the center. He touched one of the shiny black spheres that rested at the top of each chair, saw that they were attached only by cords, and carefully lifted one up with both hands.

It was a helmet, hollowed on the inside like his own leather helmet but made of hard shell. Dark glass rounded the front to cover the eyes. One of the strange ropes he'd originally thought were roots ran between the helmet and the hub.

So then, the warrior was intended to place this helmet on for protection when he drove this buggy. It was a war machine.

Immediately Billos's pulse surged. He'd found a weapon that was far more advanced than anything he or any of the Forest Dwellers could have imagined! And if he, Billos, could find a way to operate it, perhaps find a way to return it to the forests, enter it into battle against the Horde, even . . . if he could do that, the possibilities were endless. He might single-handedly save the forests!

Each thought spun through his mind as quickly as the next, which reminded him that he was trapped in a white room without the books or food or a clue how this contraption worked. And he was here because he'd ignored the warning not to touch the books with blood.

Billos took a deep breath and walked around the machine, touching and prodding the surfaces. The central hub with all the small red lights he'd first thought were eyes was as hard as stone. But when he rapped on it with his knuckles, it sounded hollow.

So, how did one operate this beast? He rounded the whole contraption twice, looking for something to control it, like reins, though he doubted he'd find reins—this wasn't an animal. Still, there were no reins, no levers, no objects of any kind. In fact, just the smooth hub and the six seats sticking out. And the red lights that had brightened when he first touched it.

Light was coming into the room from glowing squares on the ceiling, likely some kind of glass through which the sun was shining, though Billos couldn't see past them. It made sense that the red "eyes" were just crystals reflecting light from the ceiling.

Billos sighed and was about to climb into one of the seats when he noticed a thin outline, one square foot, on the hub. He touched it, pressed lightly, felt it move.

He gasped.

The square silently slid up, revealing a row of buttons on the surface beneath. Buttons with letters on each.

How was that possible? Something unseen was making this contraption move!

Magic, then. Like the books. This weapon was even more powerful than he could imagine.

He couldn't steady the tremble in his fingers as he reached for the letters. He wasn't one who could write, like Johnis, but he knew the letters Thomas had insisted every child learn. He pushed a few and stood back.

Nothing changed. But what did he expect to change? Billos then set to work pushing buttons in every conceivable order, growing more and more frustrated as the minutes dragged on.

How many combinations could there possibly be? He tried words like *go* and *start* and *wake*, but the buggy sat dumb.

An hour stretched past, maybe two. The contraption refused to respond to his touch. Yet it had opened! There was magic inside. The weapon could be activated; he just had to learn how.

But nothing he tried seemed to work. Feeling miserably defeated, Billos tried the locked knob on the main door again, then slowly sank to his seat in the corner and stared at the silent contraption.

After what felt like a very long time, he stood and approached the weapon again, pushed a few more buttons to no avail, and decided to try something new. Moving with more deliberation now, he pushed and prodded and pulled various parts of the contraption. The seats. The ropes that ran along the sides of the seats into mesh gloves. The helmets.

Nothing happened.

He climbed into one of the seats and stuck his head into the helmet. The stench of burning rubber trees, which he'd now grown accustomed to, filled his nostrils, strong again. The helmet did nothing but darken his world.

Claustrophobia began to set in. He yanked the helmet off and sat in silence. It was useless. Nothing he tried worked. Resigned to the impossibility of his predicament, Billos leaned back and closed his eyes.

Darsal would be worried. Johnis would be furious. Silvie would be plotting his death. He'd betrayed them all, but most of all he'd betrayed Darsal.

Unless he returned with the weapon. Wasn't that justification enough to ignore Johnis's warning never to touch the books with blood?

Billos opened his eyes and stared up at the pale light. What if this really was a spider and it was playing dead, waiting for him to starve to death before it consumed him like most spiders do?

He spun out of the chair, chided himself for the absurd thought, and went back to work on the buggy. But no matter what he did, no matter what he prodded or poked or pulled, nothing happened. He was still trapped in the white room with an unresponsive weapon that provided no escape.

And now he was growing thirsty. Soon the disease would set in and crack his skin. Give him a sword and a slew of Scabs to face and he could fight to the bitter end. But in this prison he was powerless.

Billos tried to push back the panic that crowded his mind. This was it? He'd been warned, and now he was going to face the consequences.

Now motivated as much by fear as curiosity, Billos threw himself into the task of making the weapon work. For many minutes that never seemed to end, he worked feverishly, covering every square inch of the contraption, pushing every button, pulling every rope.

Nothing.

He finally retreated to the corner and dropped to his rump, breathing heavy with desperation.

"Elyon," he muttered. "Please, Elyon, I swear, I swear . . . forgive me. Deliver me from this monster that has swallowed me whole, and I'll do anything. I'll follow Johnis on this blasted mission"—he rephrased—"on this mission of yours."

Nothing happened. Naturally. Billos was now beyond himself.

"I swear, I swear." Then louder. "Help me." Then in a cry of rage. "Help me, for the sake of Elyon, help me!"

ten

"What do you mean 'disappeared'?" Thomas demanded. "I give you one order, to keep an eye on one person, not even an enemy at that, and you can't follow? Can you do nothing by the book?"

Johnis and Silvie had called Darsal's name after a long stretch of silence, then barged into the bathroom and found it vacant. It only took them a minute to discover that her horse was gone too.

Two hours of frantic searching through the forest had yielded nothing. When they'd finally found Gabil, the Roush who thought of himself as a great martial artist, he was no help. "Hunter would know," Gabil had said. He'd find the Roush named Hunter. And in the meantime, they'd better get their act together. Michal wasn't going to like this, not one bit.

Now the sun was nearly gone, and they had no clue where Darsal had gone.

"We're sorry, sir. And if Darsal were the enemy, our task would have been a simple one. She's far craftier than any Scab."

"Find her!" Thomas thundered.

"She took her horse, sir," Silvie said. "We have no idea which direction she headed."

"And don't tell me that Billos is still missing."

Johnis nodded. "Yes, he is."

Thomas threw out his arms and paced, eyeing them. He was showing his hard side because it was demanded—Johnis would do no different.

"I chose you four because you're all the same in ways not even *you* knew. Each of you share the character traits I find useful in battle leaders. I knew that you would butt heads at every turn—I told my wife as much when you went missing the first time. But this . . ." He shook his head. "I didn't know I was promoting four fighters who could find trouble as easily as a blind man finds the wall!"

"I understand, sir."

"Do you?"

"I think so. It must be maddening," Johnis said.

"Really? You read me like a book, little poet. My advice is to go home and wait. There's love between Darsal and Billos. Had I known how deep their bond went . . ."

Thomas turned away and took a deep breath. "They've probably run off to have some time alone from you two. Maybe you should consider doing the same."

"No."

Johnis's retort hung in the room awkwardly.

Johnis glanced at Silvie. "I mean 'no, I don't think Billos ran off for love,' not 'no, Silvie and I shouldn't consider doing that.'"

Still awkward, he thought, and now his face was feeling flush. "Not that we *should* run off together either, I just—"

"Save it, young man," Thomas said. "It was only a passing comment to set you at ease. I can see I failed. Though it's not a terrible idea."

Silvie seemed as flustered as Johnis was. They'd always heard that Thomas of Hunter was a romantic in his own way, a true believer in the Great Romance and completely faithful to Elyon, whom all humans, even the Horde, had once loved. But his frank advice had caught them flat-footed.

A knock sounded on Thomas's door. "Come," Thomas said.

Ramos of Middle, Johnis's father, stepped in with his younger sister, Kiella. "Well, we have the whole party here," Ramos said, grinning.

"They were just leaving," Thomas said.

"Have any of you seen Karas?" Kiella asked. "I can't find her anywhere."

Thomas looked at Johnis, then his father, incredulous. "Does losing people run in your family, Ramos?"

"Not that I know, sir."

"Find them! And do it without leaving the city. Dismissed."

eleven

The Black Forest was two days northwest, according to Hunter. A week if you went straight north and ran into the Horde who were guarding the route to the Northern Forest.

"A week?"

"If you're lucky," the Roush replied. "They'll capture you the first day, and it'll take you another six to escape, if you survive. Northwest, girl, go northwest and avoid the Horde."

"What if they've shifted west?"

"Then we're in for a fight."

The little girl's huge horse plodded over the soft desert sand to the right and just behind Darsal, who led them into the night with no intention of stopping until they reached the Black Forest. She would turn the two-day journey into one. It wouldn't take Johnis long to figure out where they were going and follow. She had to get to the book and use it without interference from him!

But what if there is no book? What if there is a book, but you don't find it? What if there is a book and you find it, but you're killed for it, along with Karas?

Darsal pushed the thoughts away. Great missions require great risk. She urged her mount to quicken its pace.

They traveled in silence into the early morning hours, heading for a star that Hunter had pointed out. She thought that the Roush and Karas had run out of things to say or were sulking in silence, but a glance back told her differently.

Karas was slumped over the horse's neck, with one arm draped over each side. She was small enough to lie securely. Here Darsal had been thinking that she'd effectively silenced the girl with her imposing air of authority, when all the while Karas was snoring through sweet dreams!

Darsal leaned forward and peered over Hunter's furry head. The Roush's eyes were closed. He was leaning back on Darsal, sleeping soundly.

None of this sat well with Darsal. If she was required to endure tomorrow's hot sun without the benefit of sound sleep, so should they. Her mind drifted back to the many contests Billos had talked her into after he'd rescued her from certain death at her uncle's hand when she was eight years old.

Billos was always up for a contest. Who could stay awake the longest? Who could eat the most fire ants before their throats swelled shut? Who would be the first to pull their head from the water? Who could hang from a rope tied to a branch the longest? One-handed? Three fingers? One finger? By their necks?

She smiled in the darkness. For a period she'd made it her life's ambition to break every one of his records. And she did. So convincingly that Billos had scolded her for doing nothing but practicing to beat him.

"Is your life's ambition to beat me?" he'd demanded. "Life's not just one long contest! What's your problem?"

You, she'd thought. *You're my problem, Billos, because I owe you my life. And I want to be like you.*

She realized then that in her attempt to please him by excelling in these feats of his, she was displeasing him. Billos was bred to be a winner; anything less only frustrated him. Though she still played his games enthusiastically after that day, she stopped practicing night and day to beat him.

Darsal reached down, untied the knot that held Hunter to the pommel, and gave him a nudge with her left arm. The Roush slowly tipped over, then toppled off the horse, a ball of fur headed to the desert floor.

He landed with a soft *thud* and, amazingly, lay still for a moment before suddenly waking and floundering for footing.

Without so much as a squawk, the Roush shook his head to clear it, stumbled forward, took flight, and settled back in his former position on the horse.

He snuggled back into Darsal's stomach, sighed deeply, and settled. Two minutes later the creature was snoring again.

Darsal was tempted to try again, but she couldn't bring herself to do it. She might have captured the Roush, but that didn't mean she couldn't like him.

"I think so too," a soft voice said to her right.

She turned to Karas, who'd woken and drawn even. Darsal returned her gaze to the gentle white sand dunes ahead. It surprised her that she was glad for the girl's company. "You think what too?"

"That it's unfair for me to sleep just because I can," Karas said.

Darsal still wasn't sure what to make of the girl. Too intelligent and witty for her own good. Brave enough to follow despite the obvious danger. But above all, Karas wanted to belong. And no wonder; her mother had been killed by her father, whom Karas had just abandoned to become a Forest Dweller. The girl had no family left.

Unless Darsal was her aunt, as the girl claimed.

"What makes you think Alucard is real?" Karas asked. "I've never seen a Shataiki, have you?"

"Yes." Was she permitted to share that?

What does it matter now, Darsal? You've broken all the rules already.

"Billos, Johnis, Silvie, and I can see both the Shataiki and the Roush. Our eyes have been opened."

"Really? Why?"

Darsal shrugged. "That's more than you need to know."

"I'm risking my life to help you. Doesn't that qualify me to know what I'm getting into? Maybe my eyes should be opened too."

Darsal scoffed. "You really do think that way, don't you? That everything revolves around you. You're not helping. If anything, you're a burden."

"Exactly," Karas said. "But if my eyes were opened, I could be more of a help. Think about it."

Darsal turned to her. "You think I have the power to open your eyes?"

"Then who does?" The horses plodded. "Can you see one now?"

"A Shataiki?"

"Or a Roush."

Darsal faced forward, then snuck a peek at the fur ball leaning back against her. "As a matter of fact, yes."

Karas rode silently for a dozen strides.

"If you can't open my eyes, at least tell me why *yours* are open."

Darsal considered the request. The girl might be helpful if she knew what they were looking for.

"We're on a mission to find the seven original Books of History," she said, then quickly recounted the barest overview of the quest.

"Then you're on the right path," Karas said after a pause. "Witch used to talk about the seven books. And of Alucard, who has more under his skin than anyone realizes. Or so Witch said."

"Has what under his skin?"

"I don't know. But don't you think it was a mistake to leave Johnis and Silvie behind? You're breaking the oath."

Darsal turned away. "My oath to Billos came first."

Another pause.

"Then I admire your loyalty, Sister. And I hope I can earn yours too."

THEY RODE HARD THROUGH THE NIGHT, INTO THE MORN-ing sun, then veered northwest as instructed by Hunter, whom Karas could not see. No sign of the Horde. Or of pursuit.

Darsal pushed harder.

"If you're not going to stop and sleep, maybe you should tie yourself in so you don't fall off the horse," Karas said.

"I'm fine."

"I won't be able to lift you up by myself," she persisted.

"You don't think I've gone without sleep before? Over three days once, in a contest with Billos." Her parched lips twisted at the memory of her and Billos waking side by side under a tree, arguing about who'd fallen asleep first.

"Then we should at least bathe in the water, right?"

"She's right, you know," Hunter said. "You never know when an arrow will pierce that water bag and drain its contents. Use it while you can."

So they stripped and bathed quickly.

Darsal withdrew some jerky from the saddlebag and remounted. "Let's go!"

Karas's horse was so tall that she had to jump to reach the

pommel; then she muscled her way up and swung one leg over the saddle.

Darsal led them through the desert's blazing afternoon heat, torn between anger at Karas's persistent questions and the small comfort they provided her. Questions, questions, so many questions.

What do the Forest Dwellers eat and drink at celebrations? What's this about Thomas of Hunter coming from the Histories? What does a Roush look like? Do you really love Billos so much as to trade all the forests for him?

"Don't be a squat. It's unfair to pass judgment cloaked in a deceptively innocent question. Who said anything about trading the forests?"

"Isn't that what you're doing?" Hunter muttered.

Karas came back with yet another question. "Is *squat* a bad word?"

"No. Not necessarily. It refers to someone's height or lack thereof. It can be used for fun or for slander."

"Which way are you using the word?"

Darsal frowned. "For fun, of course."

The two horses plodded on. Midday came and went; afternoon pulled the blazing sun inexorably toward the horizon; distant clouds turned fire red until darkness shut out all but twinkling stars.

Once again Karas fell asleep, using her mount's neck as a bed. Once again, Hunter snuggled back against Darsal's belly and started to snore softly.

Alone in the dark morning hours, Darsal finally let her emotions catch up to her. The dread she'd felt at being abandoned by Billos was now swept away by a terrible sorrow. What if she really had lost him forever? She didn't know how to live without Billos. She was meant to marry him and bear his children one day, wasn't she?

And she still would . . . She would find that boy and save his thick head. And if necessary, she would teach him a lesson or two.

Then she would marry him.

Darsal saw the first Shataiki as the western sky began to lighten. At first she thought it was a dark desert shrub on the rise ahead, silhouetted by the graying sky behind. Or a rock on the horizon, because they'd passed a rare outcropping of boulders an hour earlier.

It lifted one wing, moved a foot to its left, and she thought, *A buzzard is stalking us. What does it know that we don't?*

Then the red eyes came into focus, and Darsal pulled back on her reins. Shataiki! And not just one. A dozen or so, rising from the sand dune a hundred paces ahead.

Hunter spit to one side. Darsal hadn't noticed him waking. "Their smell ruins the desert," the Roush said. "We are close."

"Sentries?"

"Yes, but I can smell more than those fourteen. Look up."

Darsal did and saw a hundred black spots circling in the dim sky.

"How far?"

"A few miles and everything will change."

"Then it's time for you to go."

"Perhaps," Hunter said.

Karas sat up, stared around, then faced Darsal. "What's going on?"

"We're there."

"We are?" Another look. "How do you know?"

"Shataiki. Ahead and above us."

Karas craned her neck and studied the sky. "Really?"

"Really." To Hunter: "There's only one thing you can do to help us now. You don't stand a chance on your own, am I right?"

The Roush didn't admit it quickly, but he could not lie. "Yes."

"Then fly back to Middle Forest and tell Johnis where we are. I have a two-day head start—if I can't accomplish what I've come for in the two days it takes him to get here, it was never meant to be. Do you follow?"

"You want me to fly?" Karas asked. "I told you, you need sleep!"

"Not you, squat. I'm talking to Hunter. Well, Hunter? What is it?"

"You're a fool to go into the Black Forest, you realize that."

"I have some bargaining chips."

"Who's Hunter?" Karas demanded.

"The Roush who's sitting on my horse. He's been with us the whole time. Now please let me finish my business with him."

"If you wanted Johnis, why not just bring him in the first place?" Hunter asked.

"Because he wouldn't have come! And if he'd come, he might have turned us back. I couldn't take that risk. Now it's too late. He'll come. Go to him."

"Are you sure you haven't lost your mind to this desert?" Karas asked.

"Yes. Hunter, I'm waiting."

"Fine. Fine, but I don't like it." He mumbled something and hopped onto the horse's head, facing them both. "The least I can do is give you two sets of eyes."

Hunter swept his wing toward Karas and whispered. "For this one, who has ears to hear and eyes to see, let her hear and see."

Karas gasped and stared wide-eyed at Hunter. "What's that?"

"I'm Hunter, the Roush that Darsal kidnapped from Middle Forest."

Karas blinked at the furry white animal. "You're real. So cute!"

"*They're* real too," Darsal said, motioning ahead at the Shataiki who stared with red eyes. "Not so cute."

Again, Karas gasped. "Shataiki!" She grabbed a bag of water from behind her and pulled it into her lap.

"You're sure about this?" Hunter asked. "I could take her with me."

"I doubt she'd go. Besides, you can't fly with her. Go. Now. You're free; go before I change my mind."

Hunter fluttered over to Karas's horse and landed on its head. "Touch my fur, cute little girl; go on, touch it."

She reached her hand out and stroked his neck lightly, eyes sparkling with wonder.

"You see, real. It's all real, everything the Horde can't see and many Forest Dwellers don't care to see. And it's all part of the real order. Elyon's order. That's his water you have, and it's a good idea. Keep Darsal alive for me until I get back with Johnis, will you?"

"Me? I will. I swear I will!"

Then Hunter leapt off the horse, spread his wings, zoomed low over the desert sand, and winged his way south.

Darsal and Karas sat on their horses, alone, facing the Shataiki, who were unfazed by this intrusion into their domain.

"Ready?"

"For what?" Karas asked.

Darsal cast her a silent look, then nudged her horse forward.

twelve

Billos awoke and found himself curled up in the corner with his cheek plastered on the hard, white floor and his saliva pooling.

He sat up, disoriented. Then he remembered where he was. Imprisoned in this white room with a useless contraption called DELL. No book, no food, no water. Abandoned by Elyon.

His desperation had grown slowly as he'd become more aware of just how confining his new environment really was. The mystery had been replaced by a predictability that offered nothing new, no matter what buttons he pushed or levers he pulled or surfaces he pried. The buggy, if indeed that's what it was, lay dormant.

There was no way out, not without a horse to kick through

the door. Maybe not even then. He'd slammed into the glass wall with his full weight and bounced back like a hollow walnut shell.

He wondered if this was hell, the place reserved for the Horde. Maybe the books were a gateway straight to hell itself. Maybe that's why Teeleh was so interested in them.

"Please, Elyon, forgive me for my hot head. I shouldn't have used the book, and I swear never to use it again if you'll save me."

But he prayed this a hundred times to no avail.

Billos pushed himself to his feet and walked around DELL again. He pushed the buttons for a few minutes, mumbling his disgust at anything so intricate and so dumb at once.

"Argh!" He slammed his hand on the lettered buttons. The glass surfaces glared black. The buggy sat like a lump. He looked around, trying his best to keep his mind but failing.

How long had it been? A day? And already he was going mad. There was nothing to do . . . but sleep.

Billos climbed into one of the seats, lay back on the cushion, and faced the glowing squares on the ceiling. Night didn't seem to come here. Not that he longed for darkness.

A shudder passed through his body. He shoved his hands into the gloves that were attached by black cords to the bed. Best he could tell, the ropes were the reins that steered the buggy, and these gloves were some kind of armor.

He pulled the battle helmet over his head and snapped the latch. Darkness swallowed him. His breathing sounded loud in his ears. The experience was rather frightful, but it was a change from the white room, and at the moment it was what he needed.

"Let's go, you haggard old beast. Do something!"

Nothing, of course.

Claustrophobia began to set in. He yanked the helmet and gloves off, rolled from the bed, and stood undecided.

He crossed to the door, kicked it with his boot, and screamed his frustration. "Open! Just open, for the love of . . ."

The door swung lazily inward.

Open?

Billos was so astonished that he stood still, unable to move. What had he done? He was free?

He threw the door open wide and stepped into a dark hallway. The door at the other end was open. He ran down the passage, feet slapping the smooth floor with each stride.

The hall opened to a larger room with a cushioned floor, unlike any he'd seen. Stuffed chairs were situated around the room in neat groupings. Against one wall stood the room's only door, this one with some letters stamped above it: EXIT.

Billos crossed to the door, heart hammering. He was free; he was going to make it. To where, he had no clue—but out. Out was what he'd needed, and out was where he was going!

He put his hand on the door and twisted. It swung easily into a dim interior. Cool air flooded his face.

Okay, okay, not the bright sunlight he'd been expecting, but he was out, right? Or was he?

The wind carried a distant voice to him. Yelling from over-head, if he wasn't mistaken.

He ran into a damp hallway with rough walls, past a curtain, into a dimly lit room with gray walls and stacks of brown contain-ers. Stairs rose on his left, and he hurried for them.

The voices grew louder. Or voice, he should say—one gruff voice expressing enough outrage to slow Billos to a timid climb.

He nudged the door at the top, saw no immediate danger, and stepped into . . . a library of some kind?

Bookcases towered on either side of a passage that led into a great room, two stories high. A large crystalline chandelier hung from the domed ceiling.

"You betrayed them, Cutes. For that I think you deserve to die, don't you?" The voice echoed from the main room. "You think your lover boy will try to save you now? I think not."

A chill rode Billos's spine. He gripped the knife tighter and crept forward on the balls of his feet. Behind him the door clicked shut. He reached back for the doorknob.

Locked.

There would be no going back the way he'd come.

"You should be thrilled that at least one of you is going to make it out of this place alive. You know that these doors are sealed with blood. Only blood can pry them open. If not yours, then whose? Hmmm? Not mine, not a chance, Cutes."

Soft crying. Muffled, definitely muffled.

Something about that voice struck a chord deep in Billos's mind. Female. Familiar.

He stopped.

Darsal?

A dozen thoughts crashed into his mind, and he knew that he was right. Darsal was not only in this place, but her life was hanging in the balance.

And lover boy? Someone else? No, never!

But what if? He'd never even considered the possibility that Darsal might fall for another man. She'd never shown the slightest interest in anyone but him since he'd killed her uncle for habitually beating her to a pulp after her parents' deaths.

The thought of losing her to another man suddenly struck him as obscene. Billos dropped the pretense of stealth and sprinted the rest of the way.

Around him rose a round atrium bordered on all sides with bookcases. A dozen vacant tables sat in the middle. Railing ran along the perimeter, separating the bookcases from the tables.

Darsal was strapped to the railing, hands tied behind her back, mouth gagged with a brown cloth. Her eyes darted to him, spread wide with fear. Then wrinkled, begging.

In front of Darsal stood a tall man dressed in black. Black hat, black trench coat, black slacks, black boots tipped in silver. Dark hair to his shoulders, smile twisted like a snake's tail, one eyebrow arched.

"Hello, Billy." He paused. "Mind if I call you Billy? It's easier to say than this Bill*os* crap. Besides, *Bill* rhymes with *will*, and that's what we're here to fix. My will, her will, we all scream for Bill's will. Kapische?"

Billos stepped toward Darsal, who looked as if she'd been beaten before being strung up. "What's going on? Who are you? You can't do this!"

"I can't. Gee whiz, oh my gosh, I'm sorry. What's your plan? We all lie down and die? 'Cause that's what happens in about five minutes if we don't kill someone. Her. Or you. I'm not volunteering, and there's no other way out."

That was the second time the man in black had suggested that there was no way out of the library. Billos glanced around—no windows or doors that he could see.

"Name's Black," the man said. "Marsuvees Black. You, Billy Boy, and me, the Black man, and Darsal-poo here have all found ourselves trapped in a magical room that will only let us out if one of us dies. So say The Powers That Be."

Billos stared at Darsal, pushing down the confusion that throbbed through his head. Confusion that unnerved him like the rest of this crazy place. Like this—he looked back at the man called Black—this human dressed up like a Shataiki.

"The Powers That Be?" he asked.

Black forced a grin. "Evil, baby. I suggest we comply. Trust me, when we do get out of this room, the world that awaits you no less than seriously rocks. Power that will make your bones quiver like a snake's tail, baby."

The man took a breath, holding his grin. "But I'll let you make the choice. Let me kill her and walk into a new life. Or pretend you can stop me and die with her. Your choice."

Billos hesitated only a moment, filled with thoughts of power that might make his bones quiver, then regained his composure and with it his backbone. He walked toward Darsal, swiveling his knife.

The man called Marsuvees Black slipped a large silver knife from a sheath Billos hadn't seen until now and stepped up to Darsal.

"Think about this, you stupid nincompoop." The man spoke with a certain uncaring that made Billos believe he could as easily kill both Darsal and him as take a breath.

For a brief moment he considered his options. The man's eyes flashed above his curved lips, inviting or threatening or both.

"No," Billos said. Then he threw reason aside and vaulted the railing, knife extended.

"No? The boy from the land of books says no?"

"I said no!" Billos launched himself at the man in a single bound that carried him much higher than he expected with ridiculous ease.

He spun once in the air and thrust out his right foot, knowing Black could not anticipate such a precise, powerful move. Truth be told, *he* could hardly anticipate it. The air was different here.

His foot swished through the air where Black . . .

Through thin air. He'd shifted? So quickly!

Billos landed on his feet and ducked in anticipation of the blow he knew would come.

Silence filled the room. Only his heart disturbed the stillness. He whipped around to his left. No one.

To the right. No one.

No Darsal. No Black. He was alone.

Billos stood straight, breathing steadily through his nostrils, knife still ready.

"Hello?" His voice echoed softly. "Hello, hello . . ."

He'd imagined it all? He was dreaming, like Thomas of Hunter had once supposedly dreamed, unable to distinguish reality from dreams?

"Hello?" he called again.

"Hello, Billossssssss."

Billos whirled. The man in black stood between two bookcases, legs spread slightly, arms crossed, head tilted down, grinning.

"Surprised?"

Billos kept his blade out, tip trembling despite his attempt to still it.

"You did well, son. Very well, I might say." The man lowered his arms and walked out into the room, scanning the ceiling. "I had to know where your heart was, you understand. If you had made any other choice, I would have left you alone to make your way in this messed-up place. Live or die, I don't—"

"Stop!"

The man faced him. Surprised.

"How did you do that?" Billos asked. "Where did she go?"

"Nowhere. She was never here. Are your ears plugged? I set

that up to test your loyalty. You showed me that you won't turn your back on those you love."

"Which does not include you. What is this place? How did you make her appear and disappear?"

The corner of Black's mouth nudged his right cheek. "I wasn't lying about the power in this world, baby. But I need you to trust me the way I trusted you."

"Trusted me? You threatened—"

"Stop!" Black thundered. Then softer, "Stop being so dense. If I'm going to partner with you, I need to know I can trust you. Can I? Because if I can't, so help me, I'll leave you to face your own demons."

Billos felt his muscles relax some. "So none of that happened?"

"In your mind, with your body—is there a difference? It happened. I gave you a choice, and you chose her over yourself. I refuse to work with anyone who isn't completely loyal."

"I don't give my loyalty easily," Billos said. "What makes you think I care about you?"

"The fact that I'm your only way out. The fact that I can give you what you deserve. The fact, Billy-boy, that you're here for a purpose. The fact that I've been waiting for you for a long time."

So then Black was good?

The man continued. "Now and then we're all confronted with a new slice of truth, an opportunity that could change everything. The realization that the brick wall in front of us isn't solid at all, if we only have the guts to run pell-mell into it."

Billos lowered his knife.

Black smiled. "What do you think, Billy-bong?"

Billos glanced around. "I don't know . . ."

"Am I good? Or am I evil?"

He thought for a moment and gave the only answer that made any sense to him. "I don't know."

Marsuvees Black smiled, teeth white, mouth pink. "I like you, boy. We're going to get along just fine."

"Where's Darsal? The real Darsal?"

"Looking for you, I would guess."

It made sense. They would all be looking for him. Wondering what had happened to the books. Johnis would be pacing a ditch into the ground, worrying, wondering what Billos knew that they did not.

But Billos didn't know enough.

"So I suppose you'd like to know what's happening," Black said.

"Fair enough, what is happening?"

Black winked. "The million-dollar question." He interlaced his fingers and cracked his knuckles. "Or should I say the seven-book question, which makes the million-dollar question look like a piece of week-old spinach on the bottom of a boot."

"Where am I?"

Black paced to his left, eyes still on Billos. "You're here, in the good old U-S-of-A. Where three of the seven books have gone conveniently missing. Do you know what the books do, Billy? Do you mind if I call you Billy?"

"My name is Billos. And no, I'm not sure I do know what they do."

The man chuckled. But it was a friendly sound that tempted Billos to grin with him.

"Well, Billos, then let me tell you. It's high time you know why we sought your help. The books are pure transparency, baby. Reality stripped of rules except those written in the books themselves. The truth. They can make truth, and they tell it the way it is—no mincing of words. No rules except those written into the books themselves."

"What does that have to do with me disappearing into the book and waking in the white room?"

"You didn't disappear into the book. You entered the book's cover, which is a different matter, you'll see. Either way, it's all real, baby, and it's all good."

He turned his head and stared at the far wall, where Billos saw a door that he didn't remember seeing earlier.

"Well, not *all* good," Black said. "In the wrong hands, the seven books could be quite a problem."

"Why all seven books?"

"Together all seven can undo any rules written into the books." He faced Billos again, light from the windows glinting in his eyes. "Their power is limitless. Which is why we need to secure them before the Dark One gets his paws on them. And we need you to help us, Billos-baby. Not Johnny-come-lately, not Saliva, not even Dorksal, although she's a close second. We were interested in *you*."

The words made Billos dizzy for a moment. These names were nearly beyond him, but he knew Black was referring to Johnis, Silvie, and Darsal.

"Why me?"

"Who's standing here now? Johnny-come-lately? Saliva? Only you had the guts to do what needed to be done to get to where the books are. Johnis played his part, don't get me wrong. But this has always been your trip, baby."

"And who's to say that *you're* not the Dark One?" Billos asked, though he was starting to think that Black had made some good points.

The man stared at him hard, surprised. "No, no, no, boy. Don't mistake my little test with Darsal for more than that. Like I've said—to the point of making me wonder if you're thicker in the head than I was led to believe—I had to know how loyal you were."

Made sense. Right?

"Then who is the Dark One?"

"The black, nasty bat, naturally. You're going to have to choose his way. Or my way. Take your pick."

"So this is all about you finding the books," Billos said.

"Before he does. Like I said, his way or my way. You either accept the fact that you were actually meant to come here and find me for the sake of the books, which is my way. Or you believe that you betrayed the others by making off with the books and entering them; that would be the nasty way of Teeleh."

"And if I choose your way?" Billos said.

"Then you bring me the four books from your reality, which will allow us to find the last three books that are lost on Earth."

"We only had three books."

"Well, you better get those three back and then find the fourth, baby. 'Cause we need all four to find the three hidden on Earth. Where I hail from."

"And why do you need me? Go get them yourself."

"You don't know? Only those from your reality can see the books here, unless all seven are together. The three you've lost can only be found by someone from your side. By you. You see, it all comes back to you. I can clap my hands and . . ."

He clapped his hands, and a book of history materialized in his right hand.

". . . presto, I have a book. Cool, huh?"

Billos blinked. "The book's cold?"

"Expression they use here. Never mind. It's an illusion, like Darsal. Unfortunately this book isn't"—he brought his hands together again and the book vanished—"real. This, however"—he snapped his fingers and a goblet appeared in his grasp—"is real. Care for a sip?"

Black lifted the glass to his lips and drank the milky substance. "Ahhh . . . Worm sludge, they call it, but it's delicious. Take a drink." He nodded at a table to Billos's right where a similar glass goblet sat, filled to the brim with the nectar.

"It'll give you the kind of power you need to finish this task of yours."

Billos hesitated, then picked up the glass. Smelled the drink. A sweet, musky odor reached up into his nostrils and stung his eyes. He felt lightheaded and pleasant. He'd had strong grog, but nothing that smelled so delicious and none that affected the mind with a single sniff.

He took a sip. The worm sludge, as Black had called it, tasted awful, much like he imagined worm sludge would taste. But it filled him with such a feeling of . . . what was it? Confidence? Power, the man had said power.

He took another sip. On second thought it wasn't so bad at all. Warmth spread through his chest and arms. Mighty fine grog at that, this worm sludge.

Black was grinning.

"So what is it, Bill? My way or his way?"

The choice seemed clear. And although Black's approach was rather unorthodox, it was compelling.

"Naturally, I'll give you more than grog," Black said. "Clap your hands, baby."

"Now?"

"Now. Put the drink down, and clap your hands together."

Billos took one more slug, set the glass down, and clapped his hands. A bolt of energy rode up his arms. Without warning, a piece of formed steel appeared in his right fist. Like a curved knife with a handle in his palm, and a tube where the blade should be.

He was so stunned by the appearance of the strange object that he nearly dropped it. He studied it in awe. He'd done this?

"How . . . how did . . ."

Black chuckled. "You like? That's what I'm talking about, baby. Magic! I call it suhupow. Short for superhuman power."

"Suhupow," Billos repeated, staring at the weapon. "What is it?"

"It's called a gun. Pull the trigger."

He assumed the small lever under the crook of his forefinger must be the trigger, so he pulled on it.

The weapon bucked in his hand, throwing it back. *Boom!* Thunder crashed overhead.

Billos yelped, dropped the weapon, and grabbed his ears. His heart pounded. "What? What happened?"

Black chuckled and nodded at a chair next to him. "You missed me."

The chair's back had a large, splintered hole in it. He'd done that? Billos looked down at the gun. Smoke coiled from the hole on one end.

"My way or his way?" Black asked again.

"What's in it for me?"

"More power than you can imagine, Billy-boy."

Billos's lips twitched in wonder. "Your way," he said.

"Very cool." Marsuvees Black snatched up the goblet of worm sludge. "I'll drink to that. Join me?"

Billos picked up his glass, now feeling altogether intoxicated and headstrong.

Black lifted his glass. "To Billos."

Billos toasted the air. "To the books."

Black: "To grace-juice, baby!"

Billos: "To the gun!"

Black threw his head back and laughed. "Drink!"

They drained their glasses as one. Then Black threw his to the ground, where it vanished a split second before striking.

"Now, let's go rule the world!"

Billos threw his glass down and watched it disappear.

He looked up, grinning so wide it hurt. "Yes, let's rule the world . . . baby!"

thirteen

The Black Forest lay in a massive depression that could not be seen until they were upon it. Even then Darsal knew that no human besides she, Johnis, Billos, Silvie, and now Karas could see it at all.

The Shataiki parted for them as they neared. "Keep the water handy," Darsal said.

"You don't need to remind me. I know how frightened it made me just a few days ago."

They urged their horses up to the depression's lip and stared over a cliff into the abyss. Black, leafless trees covered the charred ground below. Thousands of black bats perched on the branches, looking up at them.

The forest ran a mile or so in, then dipped under a huge rock lip that stretched the depression's full width. The earth swallowed up the forest. How far underground the trees grew, Darsal couldn't tell, but according to Hunter, this forest was larger than the last, and by that measure, the underground cavern had to be massive indeed.

Evidently the black trees didn't need sunlight to grow. Only the fertile soil of death.

"We're really going to go down there?" Karas asked in a voice that trembled. Finally she was showing her youth.

"It wasn't my idea for you to come."

Karas stared at a large Shataiki bat that waddled closer and settled on the lip, staring back at her with its cherry eyes. Flies, always flies around these putrid beasts. This one looked like it had more flies than fur covering its mangy body.

And the smell . . . there were no words to describe the rotting stench that clogged their nostrils. Darsal could hardly breathe through her nose, and the idea of breathing through her mouth made her sick.

None of the Shataiki seemed surprised by their presence. It was as if they'd been long expected.

"He's waiting," the Shataiki that had come closer said in a low, scratchy voice.

Karas faced Darsal and saw that the girl's lips were quivering.

"Stay close." Darsal turned her horse onto a series of switch-backs cut from the cliff. The Shataiki watched them go. Several squawked fifty meters away, but their attention was on something they fought over, not on Darsal or Karas.

The air grew warmer and even more putrid as they descended. With each step the feeling that she had made a mistake in coming here grew, and Darsal had to work a little harder to persuade herself otherwise. But she was on a rescue mission, not unlike Johnis's mission to save his mother and the girl who rode behind her.

"Darsal?"

"Quiet, Karas."

"I'm frightened, Sister."

So am I, Sister. "I'm not your sister. But stay close, and keep the water closer. You're safe with me."

The path leveled at the bottom and snaked into the towering forest. Angular branches covered with moss jutted every which way in a tangled mess, blotting out the morning sun. The rancid air turned cool and damp.

Shataiki bats screeched overhead, glaring with red eyes, following them from tree to tree.

"It's dark," Karas said.

And darker yet to come. "We'll follow the eyes."

"I'm really, really frightened, Darsal. Maybe we should go back."

"We couldn't even if we wanted to. Please, just try to be brave and keep quiet."

"Can't we talk? I think it would help."

It wouldn't hurt, Darsal decided. And the sound of Karas's voice did cut the chatter of the Shataiki—perhaps they were trying to listen in.

"Okay, tell me about how Johnis rescued you."

So Karas told her all the details as they continued into the darkening forest, step by step. The path began to descend again when they passed under a huge overhang. Their voices sounded hollow in the cavern. To think this hole had been here the whole time, harboring a more ominous threat than all of the Horde combined!

You do not belong here, Darsal.

It was Billos's doing, and for a moment she hated him for his impulsive, selfish bullheadedness. She muttered under her breath.

"What?"

"Nothing."

They'd traveled into the darkness nearly an hour, giving the horses their heads, when the sound reached Darsal. She pulled up.

"Water," Karas said.

It was only a dripping sound, but now that Darsal could hear it, she could also smell the musky, dank smell of stale water.

A flame suddenly swooshed to life a hundred meters ahead, casting an orange glow in the cavern. Karas inhaled sharply.

They were at the very edge of an underground lake with a black surface. Across the water sat a wooden platform, all too familiar to Darsal. On the platform stood a solitary Shataiki, larger than the rest, and in his claw he held a large torch.

"Alucard," Karas guessed.

"Alucard."

They could see the ceiling now, hewn from the rock, jagged and dripping water from long stalactites. The drops of water fell to the lake's surface and sent out ripples—the sound they'd heard.

The path snaked around the lake, barely visible between the gnarly trees and the stagnant water. Darsal turned her horse right and forced it forward. Without trees to support them over the lake, thousands of Shataiki now perched on the trees that ran the lake's perimeter, staring with beady eyes. So many that Darsal thought the cavern's orange glow might be caused in part by the eyes, not just the torch.

Without moving, except to face them as they rounded the lake, Alucard watched them come. And then they were in the mud before the platform, eye to eye due to their being mounted on horses.

The beast stood nearly twice as tall as most Shataiki, and his skin was more than twice as mangy. Fur worn thin to reveal his skin beneath. He looked very old, if age was something that could be judged by how haggard a beast looked. His upper lip hung down on either side of his snout, like a sad hound that held a long stick supporting a flaming torch.

Only *this* hound gazed at them with furious red eyes, not dog eyes.

A centipede scurried across the bat's brow and across its upper cheek before vanishing into the beast's ear. Darsal imagined a nest inside and shivered.

"Only one of you," Alucard finally said in a low, wet voice. Saliva trailed off his snout and dripped to the ground. "And this traitor."

"I'm here on my own," Darsal said. "Armed with water—"

"Silence!" the bat snapped.

Darsal flinched.

"Does this look like your home? It's your tomb."

"Then it'll be your tomb as well," Darsal said, gathering the last reserves of her courage. She cast a quick glance to her right at Karas. The girl was shaking.

Eyes back on Alucard. "I've come to make you a deal."

That set the bat back a few moments.

"I don't make deals with my enemy," he said.

"You did with Tanis. Or was that Teeleh? You don't have the power to deal like that greater monster?"

"I could have you killed with the slightest move of my hand."

Darsal glanced at the beast's sharp, curved claws. For the last two days she'd thought about the proposition she would now voice, and however preposterous, however blasphemous, however treacherous it sounded, she saw no way around it.

But first she had to know if Alucard had one of the books.

"You can't kill me," Darsal said. "Not if you want the books."

"I'll do what pleases me in my home."

"You're not just a pawn of that bigger beast, Teeleh?" Darsal asked. "I assumed you do only what pleases him."

No response.

"You have another one of the books, safeguarding it for Teeleh, I imagine." Darsal didn't know this, of course, but she said it as if it were well-known. "I have three. But the three I have are with Billos, and Billos can only be gotten to via the book in your possession. Are you following me?"

"You've lost the books in your possession? You're even more foolish than I thought. You have nothing to bargain with."

"I do have something. I have your desire for the three books that Billos has. I can get them. But I need your book to do it."

So now it was out there. And judging by Alucard's stillness, he was interested.

"So Billos used the books. Did he open them?"

"No."

"You saw this?"

"I saw him touch the cover of one book with blood and vanish with all three." She paused. "What would have happened if he had opened a book?"

"You don't know? No, of course you don't. You're just a spoiled young warrior pretending to be important. Why he would choose you to match wits with me and the Dark One is beyond comprehension."

So Alucard knew who the Dark One was.

"Then tell me, what would happen if Billos opened a book?"

"It would depend. There were four books here: one with the Horde, one with Teeleh, one with me, and one with the Roush. Gather all four, and they would create a breach into the lesser reality where the last three books are hidden. But there is no way for him to return here with the books. Unless he has all four from this reality."

"He had only three, yet he went. I saw him."

"He's not where he might think he is."

Darsal pondered this but couldn't wrap her mind around the scope of these realities he suggested.

"So you've gone? You can tell me what to expect?"

"I've been to where I assume your friend went by touching the book with blood. But I would need all four books to go to Earth." Alucard slowly smiled, but offered no further explanation.

"So you need four books to go where you want to go?" Darsal questioned. "Which is different from where Billos went, because he only had three. So where has Billos gone?"

Alucard's response came slowly and carefully. "To a place of unlimited opportunity."

"Then that's what I have to offer you," Darsal said. "Three more books and yours back after I retrieve Billos's. They would have my neck for making this deal with you, and frankly I'm not sure I can offer it much longer. Any minute and I'll decide to give my life up instead of the books. Which will it be?"

"You expect me to believe that you'd give up the four books for one piece of meat?"

"He's not a piece of meat," Karas said, speaking up with a thin voice. "That's the difference between you and them. They appreciate every life; you don't."

"The traitor has stopped trembling long enough to speak," Alucard said.

"From what I gather, you're the one who turned your back on Elyon."

"Shut up, Karas," Darsal snapped.

"That would make you the traitor," the little girl said.

Alucard whipped his head back and roared, an earsplitting howl that crackled with rage.

The roar rang, then echoed. Silence filled the cavern.

"Wouldn't it?" Karas said.

Had she lost her mind?

"Do not speak that name in my home," Alucard snapped. "It makes me doubt you. Why should I agree with someone who defiles my home?"

"She's a young child; ignore her. I'm the one you're speaking to. And you can trust me because I would give my life for this 'piece of meat' named Billos."

Alucard regarded her with an expression hidden by red, pupilless eyes. The centipede slid out of his ear and disappeared into a patch of mangy black fur.

"Yes, you would die for him, wouldn't you?"

He thumped the wooden platform with his stick. Three Shataiki flew in from the side and disappeared into a hole behind the dock. Into the lair, not unlike the one Johnis had entered at Teeleh's lake.

"And I'll give you that opportunity," the beast said.

Darsal's pulse pounded, as much from the anticipation of accomplishing her first objective as from a gnawing fear.

"How many big bats like you are there?" Karas asked. The tremble was gone from her voice.

Alucard just stared at her.

"Why do you want to go where Billos has gone?"

Darsal didn't think the bat would entertain such simple questions from a little girl. "Karas . . ."

"I am Shataiki!" the beast snapped.

"And that bothers you?" Karas pushed.

"Did it bother you to be Horde?"

"No. I was too deceived. Are you saying you want to bathe in the lakes and make amends with Elyon?"

Alucard's neck stiffened, and his lips pulled back to reveal sharp, crusted fangs.

"Sorry, you didn't want me to speak Elyon's name. I forgot."

The beast's coat quivered, sending flies that Darsal hadn't noticed buzzing. "This is my home." He seemed to force each word out, one by one.

"But you don't want it to be?" Karas persisted.

For a long time Alucard just glared at her, and Karas stared back, though her shaking hands betrayed the state of her nerves. The entire forest had become deathly quiet.

When the beast spoke, his voice was nearly a growl. "Human," he said. "What I do, I do for a purpose beyond your understanding. A purpose that serves Teeleh well."

Darsal remembered something that Gabil, the Roush, had said before. That all Roush were in wonder of humans, the beings Elyon had fashioned after himself. Maybe jealous in a friendly sort of way. Now, looking at Alucard, she knew that Shataiki were also jealous. A bitter, spiteful hatred for being less than Elyon and human.

One of the three Shataiki who'd descended into the lair emerged. Darsal's horse shifted under her. The bat settled on the platform, clacked across to Alucard, and held out a leather bag.

"Take it out and put it between us."

The bat withdrew a filthy bundle. Careful so as not to touch its contents, he peeled back the dirty rags and exposed an old, green book bound in red twine. He set the half-exposed book on the wood planks. *The Stories of History.*

Darsal's fingers tingled. The fourth book. Her gateway to Billos. Her concern for any danger they had walked into fell away. It was all she could do not to slice her finger right then and there and thrust it against the ancient leather cover.

"Swear to me on your life that you will bring back all four books, and I will give you safe passage from here," Alucard said.

"I swear," Darsal said, only half-believing herself.

"If you do not, either you or Billos is mine. My choice."

"Yes."

"Then seal the oath with the book."

What did he mean?

"An oath made over the books is binding. You cannot break it and live. Did you expect me to take your unbound word?"

The revelation took some of Darsal's wind away. But now she was committed.

"Not a good idea," Karas said.

"Quiet!"

Darsal dismounted, walked to the book, placed one hand on

the cover, and swore to return all four to Alucard or forfeit her life. And Billos's, though she wasn't sure she could swear for him.

She wrapped her fingers around the book and stood. "May I?"

"Take it," Alucard said.

He stared at her for a few moments. Without another word, he turned and clacked away from them. The torchlight wavered, then snuffed out, leaving them in darkness. Surrounded by a sea of red eyes in the trees.

"What have you done?" Karas asked.

fourteen

The library led to a stone tunnel, which in turn led to a flight of rock-hewn steps, which finally ended at a trapdoor in the floor of a small cabin.

Marsuvees Black led Billos out of the cabin and down a canyon, always staying one step ahead. Turning back now and then to deliver his nuggets of truth.

"Life's what you make it, boy. A clean sheet every day."

"Do you like mustard? Keeps the mind sharp."

"They're all enemies, Billos. Don't trust them. The nicer they talk, the worse they are."

"You ever stake anyone through the heart, Bill*os*?"

Half of the comments made no sense, but all of them intrigued Billos.

To think that all along their search for the books was designed to take him through the books to this magical place where you could snap your fingers and have them filled with steel.

Billos tried it again and was immediately rewarded with a gun. He twirled it in his hand, relishing the very feel of this amazing weapon that could scare people with its bang and destroy objects some distance away with its suhupow. And to stow it you simply . . .

Billos threw the gun at the earth and watched it vanish. Amazing.

"Find me the books, and the world is yours," Black said, winking. He was both frightening and intoxicating at once. "Try snapping the fingers of your other hand."

Billos did. This time a rose appeared.

"To seduce the women, my friend."

He smelled the rose, felt it tickle his nose, then threw it into oblivion. "Ha! Is there any limit to this suhupow?"

"Not if you make it to the top. Follow me; I'll show the way."

They passed through a forested region and came out on a cliff overlooking a village. The structures were unlike any he'd ever seen. They were more square and smoother, and the roads between them were black, perfectly straight.

"Welcome to Paradise," Black said. His face twitched. "The little town that could. But that'll all change. This is where I leave."

"Leave? I don't know this place."

"Didn't stop me; shouldn't stop you. Like I said, you have to find the books on your own, then bring them to me."

"Down there?"

"Maybe they're there, maybe not. But down there is where you start. Practice. This little hole is full of conspirators who'll have you fooled the moment they open their mouths, if you let them. Think of Paradise as your final test. *Comprende?*"

"Comprende." Whatever that meant.

"Watch out for impostors. Shape-shifters. Brats who pretend to be your best friends. Conspirators, the bunch of them."

Billos walked to the edge of the cliff and studied the tiny forms of villagers walking down the main street. "Conspirators."

"Bring me the books. I need four, but I'll take three for now. See you on the dark side, baby."

"All of them are evil?" Billos asked, turning back.

But Marsuvees Black was gone. Vanished.

For a moment Billos felt alone. But just for a moment. Because then he snapped his fingers, watched a steel gun materialize in his hand, and he felt very much at peace.

He stowed the gun with a flip of his wrist, cracked his neck, faced the village below, and headed down to Paradise.

DUST BLEW OVER THE STREET THAT RAN DOWN THE MIDDLE of Paradise. Billos stopped at a sign that read, WELCOME TO PARADISE, POPULATION 545, and stared ahead in wonder. Words could hardly describe what he saw. *Suhupow, everywhere suhupow!*

The road he stood on was rock hard, perfectly formed from a

black substance that looked to have been melted and laid down in one long strip. But more stunning than this finely crafted road were the buggies that traveled on top of it. Painted in different colors with black wheels to roll over the road, they moved without horses, without any beast pulling or pushing. With suhupow and suhupow alone.

Billos felt like a child of wonder more than a warrior who'd trained his whole life to kill the Horde. What would Darsal say of Paradise? He strode down the yellow dash in the middle of the road, not bothering to wipe the crooked grin from his mouth.

Two things were now clear to him. No, three things: First, he'd made the right choice to enter the Book of History, which had, if he wasn't mistaken, taken him into history itself. Second, the mission was really about Billos's helping Marsuvees Black find the Books of History, which were invisible to all but him here in the histories. And third, this critical mission depended on his skill, his intelligence, his craftiness—his ability to defeat the enemy and find what no other man could find.

It's your turn to follow me into hell, Johnis. Shut your flapper, Scrapper, and stay close behind. Not a peep, because I don't have time to babysit every time you cry out in fear. You too, Silvie.

Darsal, step up here by my side. It's our turn. It's our turn to trip, baby.

A thought occurred to him: he wasn't dressed for the occasion. This brown tunic he'd worn from Middle Forest felt out of place. Ahead a man dressed in blue slacks and a brown hat swept dust from the sidewalk, paying him no mind. The establishment behind him had a large red sign that read SMITHER'S BARBEQUE.

On a whim, Billos snapped his fingers. The gun materialized in his hand. He shoved it into his pocket, thought of a hat, touched his head, and snapped again.

Shade covered his head. He pulled off a black, broad-rimmed hat that looked just like the one worn by Marsuvees Black. Replacing the hat, he snapped his fingers again and was immediately rewarded with black pants and a black trench coat. He was now suited for battle in the histories.

Two men sat on a bench next to the worker who swept the sidewalk. One of the buggies, a red one, rolled past him on four black wheels, purring as it swished by. It belched at him angrily, the sound of a goose honking. Billos stepped to one side and placed his hand on the gun, which was now tucked in his belt. But the machine didn't attack.

Crafty conspirators, every one of them. The Horde of the histories. He had to move among them without raising an alarm until he was ready. Practice, Black had said.

He couldn't very well just start slaying them with the gun, could he? They would likely pour out of the buildings armed with swords. Or, worse, armed with guns. Did they also have these magical weapons?

Billos had fought off the Horde in full combat, killing them with a skill he'd developed over many years, growing to be a man of seventeen. The enemies sitting on the bench and the one sweeping the porch didn't appear hostile, but Billos might prefer to face a dozen armed Scabs at the moment. At least the Horde didn't wield suhupow.

One of the men on the porch beneath the Smither's Barbeque sign faced him and tilted his hat back. Billos mistook the gesture as an aggressive move and very nearly pulled out his gun. But instead he shoved his anxiety down, lowered his head, and strode on as if at complete ease. He saw that he still wore his brown boots from the forest; they looked out of place under the black slacks. But he wasn't here to impress them with his sense of good fashion.

"Howdy, partner. Can I help you?"

Billos drilled him with a stare, walking on. "Can you? That depends."

The other man looked at him cautiously, as if measuring him for a casket, then relaxed. He considered something then dismissed it. Or was being sly.

"Well, if it's a drink you want, I'm just opening."

The two men rose, eyeing him curiously. No weapons that Billos could see. They followed the man who'd been sweeping inside, leaving Billos on the street.

He glanced around and saw that he was alone. But he wasn't so easily fooled. The enemy was undoubtedly peering at him by the dozens, lying in ambush.

Suddenly unnerved, Billos sprinted to the alley between Smither's Barbeque and the establishment next to it, All Right Convenience. Both were names that meant nothing to him.

116

He pulled up under the eaves, backed against the wall, and immediately chided himself for running. Such an obvious reaction was sure to put them on guard. He withdrew the gun and stared at it.

He sniffed the tube. Looked down the hole. It was a fantastic weapon that he would take with him back to the forest. They would immediately promote him to general with such a gun.

"Hello?"

Billos spun to his left, gun leveled. A young boy with blond hair stood behind the building, staring at him with round, green eyes.

"You don't need that," the boy said.

Billos lowered the barrel; no need to be too obvious. "You startled me."

"He's lying, you know."

"Who is?"

"The Dark One. Black."

So it was starting already—Billos had to tread very carefully. This boy not only knew of Marsuvees Black but was conspiring to undermine him.

"You think I don't know that?" Billos said.

"I think your mind is too full of yourself to know that," the boy said. "I think you would betray Elyon in favor of the Dark One. It wouldn't be the first time."

The boy seemed to know of his mission to retrieve the missing Books of History, which made him even more dangerous. A bead of sweat broke from Billos's brow and snaked down his temple.

"You're wrong. I would never betray Elyon. Do you know where the books are?"

The boy just stared at him, a clear sign that he knew more than he was saying.

"You're going to break his heart," he finally said. "All dressed up like the Dark One, swinging that gun around. Do you plan to kill us all?"

Billos didn't know how to respond to such direct threats, so he filled the empty space with small talk. "What's your name, boy?"

"My name?" See, even here the boy was being coy. "You can call me Samuel. You should give me the gun. The power you have didn't come from Elyon."

Billos turned away, gun cocked by his side. This small viper draped in bright colors was death. But the gun was too loud and would warn the others that the battle had started. He eased his hand closer to the knife strapped on his thigh.

"Well, Samuel, since you obviously know more than I do, you won't have trouble believing that I'm secretly working *against* the Dark One. And I would like you to help . . ."

He brought the knife around midsentence, putting his full weight into a throwing arc that would land the blade in the boy's throat and silence him before he could warn the others.

But the boy was gone.

Billos held the knife back and searched the alley. He was alone. The boy had snuck around the building while his attention was diverted. A slippery snake.

Which meant that Billos's hand was now forced. This Samuel would warn the others. Billos had to earn their trust and take the battle to them or risk an ambush. Thomas had taught them well—the best defense was often a forward attack, right down their throats.

He stowed the gun and the knife, hurried around the corner, and leapt up the steps that led into Smither's Barbeque. They might be crafty, as Black had warned, but he was craftier.

fifteen

Darsal broke from the Black Forest just behind Karas, who'd taken the lead this time despite Darsal's warning to get behind. The girl couldn't temper her desire to be out of this putrid black hole.

"There it is!" Karas cried, looking up at the cliff and beyond to the blue sky. She kicked her horse into a gallop, and Darsal followed.

The green book bound in red twine sat in her saddlebag, begging to be used, and use it she would. As soon as they cleared the danger presented by the Shataiki.

Black bats rimmed the cliff, peering down, squawking, but otherwise they presented no threat. Alucard had kept his word. The fact that he could only gain through this trade wasn't lost on

121

Darsal, but neither was the fact that she'd done what was necessary to follow Billos. They would work a way out of their troubles together.

Karas didn't need to urge her mount onto the switchbacks that led to the desert above them. The horse surged up the incline, leaning into each step.

Now that she had the book, Darsal had to consider what course to take with the girl. In hindsight, she might have asked the Roush to wait in the desert and escort the girl back to the forest. As it was now, she would have to send Karas back alone with all the water and clear directions.

The girl knew the desert, after all, and it had been her choice to follow.

Darsal galloped past the girl into the desert as soon as they spilled over the lip. "Go!" They rode hard for twenty minutes before she finally eased up to give the horses a rest.

"Not fun," Karas said. "This whole business is reckless."

"Welcome to life in the forests."

"Thank you for making my point. We're in the desert, not the forest."

Darsal grunted. "We'll stop in the outcropping for a proper rest," she said.

An hour later the large outcropping rose before them, and Darsal's palms began to sweat with the anticipation of cutting her finger and thrusting the blood against the book's cover.

"You're not afraid?" Karas asked, breaking a long spell of silence.

She'd already told Karas how Billos had vanished. "Like I said, life in the forests. We live with fear, little girl."

"Sounds like the Horde."

A dozen boulders towered four times the height of their horses ahead, surrounded by one or two score smaller rocks. It would make for an ideal camp; she would have to remember its location.

"I think I should come with you, Sister," Karas said.

"Don't be ridiculous."

"Why not?"

"For starters, I don't know where I'm going. For all I know, Billos vanished into oblivion. And regardless of where it is, getting back must not be easy or Billos would have done so already. We could get stuck."

"We?"

"Billos and I."

"And me?"

Darsal sighed. "It wasn't my idea for you to—"

"I don't care if it wasn't your idea!" Karas blurted. "I'm here, aren't I?"

Darsal glanced over, surprised by the emotion in Karas's voice. Tears misted the girl's eyes.

"I followed you because I saw my mother in you. And I miss my mother! Now you're just going to throw me away like a dirty rag?"

"That's not what I'm doing. If anything I'm trying to protect you!"

"Then protect my heart as well. You don't think I'm worthy to stay with you? Ask Johnis if I was helpful in saving him."

The words stung, and Darsal wasn't sure why. What was this one small girl in the grand scheme of things? It wasn't that Darsal had no heart, only that she'd learned to protect it or suffer with every blow. And in their battle with the Horde, the blows came nearly daily.

Still, she couldn't deny that there was something special about Karas.

"What good is your heart if you're dead?" she asked. "You have to get back to the forest, where Thomas can protect you."

"I'll get lost in the desert!"

"You know the desert well enough."

"I was just rescued from the desert. I hate the desert!"

"And you hate oblivion any less?" Darsal guided her horse through a wide gap between two of the largest boulders and pulled up in the shade beyond. "Look, maybe you are my niece. If so, I have an obligation to protect you. The Roush Hunter knows you're out here. Johnis is probably already on the way. They'll send out a hundred Roush to spot you from the air and take you home. Am I just stupid, or does that seem the safest for you?"

"I'm afraid to go alone. Please, Dar—"

The word caught in her throat, and Darsal looked back to see what had stopped her.

Three Scabs on horses filled the gap behind Karas. Another to her side with a long spear pressed against her neck. For a brief moment Darsal's mind went blank. Then the survival reasoning that Thomas had drilled into his Guard screamed through.

How? Knowing how your enemy gained the advantage they had might offer a clue as to how to undo that advantage.

Why? Knowing why you allowed your enemy to gain the advantage will aid you in not repeating the same mistake.

What? What then should you do in response to your disadvantage?

All of this, in a few scarce moments, of course, or disadvantage would become disembowelment.

The answers were painfully obvious. The wind was blowing east, which explained why the horses hadn't picked up on the Horde stench. These Scabs had probably followed their tracks and holed up here for an ambush.

As to why Darsal had been so careless: she'd been completely distracted by the book. And by Karas.

Darsal's heart thundered. What to do?

There were only four Scabs, but with Karas under the blade, the girl's chances for survival were slim. Darsal had two knives and a sword. She was already considering their use, but in the next moment the situation went from difficult to impossible.

Her horse shifted nervously under her as two more mounted Scabs stepped into the clearing from behind the boulders opposite her.

"Move and she dies," the Scab with the spear growled.

He was a massive man, with muscles that coiled around his

arms like ropes. A giant who looked like he might actually make
a worthy adversary by himself.

The Scab grinned wide, exposing two shiny brass teeth.

"Come to Papa."

sixteen

Billos stepped into Smither's Barbeque, nerves strung to the snapping point, walking casually as if strolling into this establishment was something he'd done a thousand times before.

But his eyes scanned every detail, and his right hand hovered over the gun that formed a lump in his trench coat. Like the view of the village's exterior, the guts of this eatery were stunning. Glowing lamps hung from the walls, but as far as Billos could see, there were no flames. Glass. So much smooth, clear glass that Billos wondered if the histories were made from glass. Mugs, cups, lamps, windows . . . all glass.

And colors everywhere, red and blue and yellow, paintings and small statues, boxes and tables and lights; even the floor was red. All colored. The wood was carved in the most intricate and seamless fashions, curls and ovals and edges that looked sharp enough to cut meat. Almost as if they wanted him to think they were artisans rather than warriors. Crafty.

But he wouldn't be so easily fooled. Marsuvees Black was probably watching his every move at this very moment.

The man who'd invited him in for a drink stood behind a counter, drying glasses.

"What can I get you?"

Billos stared at him for a moment, checking for weapons. When he saw none that he recognized, he walked up to the counter and asked for the most common of drinks.

"Do you have blue plum wine?"

The man glanced at the other two, who were standing around a large, green table, pretending to be interested in colored balls that they struck with wood poles. It occurred to Billos that the sticks could be weapons. He would have to keep an eye on them.

"Blue plum wine, huh? No, no, I don't suppose I have any blue plum wine."

Hearing laughter in the man's tone, Billos decided that he should play the confident rabble-rouser to win their trust. Some men respected barbs more than sweet talking.

"Then what kind of grog do you have in this hole?" he demanded.

The man's eyebrow arched. "Grog? How about a light ale?"

"Ale, then!" Billos slapped his hand on the counter. He knew ale, of course, but he didn't know how putting a light inside of it might affect its taste. He'd tasted Horde ale once and had nearly thrown up. Hopefully this so-called "light ale" wasn't as bad.

"Ale," the man said, dipping his head once.

"You have no women in this village?" Billos asked, walking around the counter, looking for their hidden weapons.

"The village is full of women. All taken, I would say."

He walked up to a tall glass box, glowing red and blue with a picture of gold plates on the front. It read Jukebox and emanated the strangest music he'd ever heard. No sign of musicians.

A man began to sing from within the box, and Billos stopped. *A man is hiding in the box, singing. What kind of strategy is this?* Three men behind him now; one hidden in the box, singing to draw his attention.

Crafty, but he wouldn't let on that he was aware of their ploy.

"One ale," the server said.

Billos returned to the counter and lifted the mug of amber ale. "Thank you."

"Name's Steve," the man said, sticking out his hand.

Billos took it. "Billos," he said.

"Glad to meet you, Billy. This here's Chris and Fred."

"Bill*os*," Billos repeated, then remembered that Black had called him Billy as well. "Billy. Billy is fine." He nodded at the others, who watched him cautiously and dipped their heads.

"What brings you to Paradise?" the one called Steve asked.

Black, Billos wanted to say. "Johnis," he said instead, hoping to catch the man off guard.

"Johnny? Johnny Drake?"

"You've heard of him?" Billos asked.

"He was through here a few months ago and then disappeared. You friend or foe to Johnny?"

"Friend, of course."

"Then I suggest you find Samuel. But we don't want any trouble. We've had our share."

There was trickery afloat here. He'd already found Samuel, who was clearly the enemy. And that put Johnis and maybe the rest of them in the same camp. Like Black had said, conspirators who pretended to be your friends.

"Do you read books here?" he asked.

The man glanced at the others again, this time unsure.

"Books. Sure. Are you okay?"

"Why wouldn't I be? What kind of books, if you don't mind me asking?"

The man in the jukebox stopped singing.

"All kinds of books," Steve said. "You sure you're okay?"

Billos saw them then, all three Books of History sitting high on a bookshelf behind the counter next to some old bottles, as if they'd been there for some time.

He felt his muscles tense, then immediately removed his eyes from the shelf and forced himself to relax. This could only be the final confirmation that Black was right about Paradise. He might actually be in Teeleh's lair as it appeared in history.

Billos lifted his mug and drank deep, stilling his trembling hand. At any moment they would make their move, he was sure of it. But even as the cool nectar ran down his throat, he knew their every intention, their exact locations, and precisely how he would dispatch them.

"Think of Paradise as your test," Black had said.

In that moment a supreme confidence settled over Billos. For the average warrior, Paradise might be a test of champions, but he would show them all that for Billos of Southern, battle came as naturally as a stroll along the lake.

He loved Black, and he loved the power Black had given him, and he loved Paradise, the village in which he would prove once and for all that he was worthy of both Black and the power.

"Easy, man."

Billos drained the last of the drink and slammed the mug on the counter. He drilled Steve with a hard stare. "We can do this the easy way, or if you insist on playing coy, the hard way. But I must warn you, I'm better than all four of you put together."

The man blinked. "Four? What are you talking about?"

"The man in the jukebox. He'll be first. Give me the books, and I may let you live."

The man blinked. Crafty indeed, playing his deception to the bitter end.

"Hold on, son. You've got this all wrong. I don't know what you think you're doing here or who sent you, but it's wrong. We've had our share of trouble, but Johnny took care of that. Now . . ." Steve took a breath. "I suggest you take your black wannabe duds out of here and hit the road before someone gets hurt."

A new voice spoke behind Billos. "Everything okay, Steve?"

Billos froze. Steve glanced past him toward the door. "Morning, Jerry."

Billos slipped his hand under his trench coat, felt the cool steel at his fingertips, and spun around. A man dressed in blue stood in the open doorway. He wore a brass star on his chest and a gun on his hip. Jerry. A warrior.

Jerry's eyes shifted to Billos's hand under his trench coat. His hand reached for the gun that hung at his waist. Billos moved then, while he still had the upper hand. He jerked out the gun from which the suhupow came.

The man in blue grabbed for his own gun, and Billos threw himself to the right, pulling the lever as he moved.

Boom! The gun bucked in his grasp.

He saw the man spin around with the suhupow's impact; then Billos was on the ground, rolling to his right. He had to assume they would unload their own suhupow immediately, but moving would make him a hard target.

The man in the jukebox must be next. Surprisingly, he began to sing again, an odd, devious response to the obvious danger his partners were in. Surely he'd heard the loud discharge over his own crooning voice.

And this time, a woman joined in. There were *two* assassins in the box?

Billos came to one knee, pointed his gun at the jukebox, and pulled the lever four times. *Boom, boom, boom, boom!* The contraption exploded in a colorful shower of glass. Smoke coiled to the ceiling.

The man's and woman's voices caught in their throats. Both dead.

Now Billos was on his feet and running to his left. He leveled the suhupow at the two men bearing the stick-weapons and sent them both reeling back with two blasts. This left only the one behind the counter.

Steve.

Billos whirled and brought his gun to bear on the wide-eyed man, who was just now bringing a large metal weapon with twin tubes up from under the counter. A massive gun.

Boom! Billos sent him flying.

He held the gun steady and turned around, ready for anyone else who wanted a piece of Billos of Southern. But there was no one. His ears rang, his heart pounded, but otherwise he was surrounded by silence.

And six dead bodies, including the two in the jukebox. Dead by Billos.

"What do you make of that?" he muttered, then added, thinking of Marsuvees Black, "Baby."

A voice reached him from outside the establishment, words he couldn't make out. Other voices joined in, yelling now.

He'd awoken Paradise.

Let the fight begin.

seventeen

"COME TO PAPA."

Darsal had never encountered a Scab who seemed so cocky, but she could see why Papa was sure of himself. He was twice as big as she, had a blade against Karas's neck, and stood with five of his peers bearing down on one fighter and a child.

If Billos were here, they wouldn't have hesitated. But Billos had abandoned her, forcing her into this impossible situation.

Why hadn't Papa just killed Karas and taken up the fight with Darsal?

"Are you going to just stand there, flashing your big brass teeth, or are you going to be a man and kill us?" Darsal asked.

The Scab tilted his head, face bright and brash despite his gray eyes. "Witty are we? Good. This desert could use a lively hostage to ease the boredom."

"Just kill them as we agreed," one of the other Scabs said.

Papa shot him a stern glance. "*If* they resist, we said. This fighter hasn't touched her sword." To Darsal: "What brings you so deep into the desert with this child?"

A large Shataiki bat flapped and settled on the rock over his head.

"Him," Darsal said, looking up.

Papa followed her eyes. Faced her again. "A rock?"

"The Shataiki. You don't see it?"

"Kill them," another grunted. "No good ever came of playing with one of them. She's a viper."

"Perhaps, but even a viper can break the monotony of traveling with you, Bruntas. I would guess this one fighter could kill you with both hands tied behind her back. Care for a wager?"

"Kill the child, and you have your wager," Bruntas snapped.

Papa's grin vanished. He spit to one side. "I don't kill children."

"She's diseased!"

"She's a child!" Papa thundered.

"And you're a fool."

Papa swiveled his spear away from Karas's neck and whipped it next to his comrade's neck. "Better than a dead fool."

Darsal had never imagined, much less witnessed, a Scab defending a Forest Dweller. Either way, Papa had shown her his soft underbelly and removed his threat from Karas in one foolish move.

Darsal could attack now, but not without endangering Karas. So she kicked her horse in the flanks, driving it against Karas's mount. Before Papa could react, both horses bolted into the center of the sandy clearing.

A second Shataiki landed on the rocks above them, squawking. They were still surrounded and outnumbered, but Karas was out of reach. At least for the moment.

Papa grinned, attention back on them. "Smart," he said, fanning out with the others to form a circle of six around them. "A viper indeed."

Darsal raised both hands. "I don't want trouble."

"Then cut your own wrists, wench," the one called Bruntas growled.

There was no winning here, Darsal knew. Not without the book. The Scabs would eventually kill them both. Regardless of Papa's empathy for children, Horde law would end their lives.

"Bruntas, that is your name? I could kill you from here with a flip of my wrist. Papa knows that, but you're too stupid to realize it. Am I wrong?"

The Scab blinked. Darsal moved then, while their minds were on her words. Both hands flashing to her hip-sheaths, withdrawing a knife from each. She let them fly forward in the manner Silvie had taught her.

The blades took Bruntas and the Scab next to him in the necks. Darsal already had her sword out, spinning her horse to face the Scabs behind her. She slapped Karas's mount as she turned.

"Run for the gap!"

Karas drove her horse at the two flailing Scabs.

Darsal bolted at two others, screaming her guts out. Instead of going after both with her sword, she ducked under one of their blades and plowed her horse into theirs. Both backpedaled, snorting.

The second Scab had a spear, but the weapon was hardly more than a beating stick at this close range. Darsal struck the nearest warrior with her sword, spun it once, and drove it into the second.

"Darsal!" Karas's cry cut through the desert air.

The girl's warning told her two things: that the girl had not fled as she'd ordered, and that Papa was now bearing down on her.

She snatched the spear from the second Scab, who was now falling from his horse, twisted in her saddle, and hurled it with all her strength. She was halfway through the hurl before adjusting her sword to take out the Scab rushing her.

The blade struck him in his chest, but his momentum carried him crashing into her. They toppled to the ground as one.

She struggled to disengage the heavy, dead Scab who'd landed on top of her and finally succeeded, only to find Papa standing over her, sword extended.

"Good fight, Forest Dweller. But I'm afraid it's come to an end."

And he is right, Darsal thought. Her own sword lay on the sand, five paces away; her horse, which carried her other sword, had bolted across the clearing, taking the book with it.

This behemoth of a Scab had a blade inches from her throat.

"Do you know who the girl is?" Darsal asked.

"No. Should I?"

"Karas. Daughter of Witch."

Papa continued to grin, but his face suddenly appeared wooden. "Is that so? I had heard she was missing. Then I'll let Witch decide what to do with her."

"No," Karas said behind him. "You won't."

She had dismounted and was walking toward them carrying nothing but the book.

"And if you know what's good for you," she said to Papa, "you will bathe in some of the water we've brought and cleanse your mind of the disease."

"Stay back," he snapped.

Karas stopped and looked up at him. "Are you going to kill her?"

"I have to. If you really are the daughter of Witch, you know that." Then he added to make it clear, "Not that I don't *want* to kill her, mind you."

Karas tossed the Book of History toward Darsal. "Then at least let her die in peace." The book thudded to the sand, two feet away.

Darsal's mind spun through her alternatives and settled on the only course of action that made sense.

"Thank you." Slowly she reached her hand to Papa's sword. "Please, let me die with blood on the book. It's the only way I can find paradise."

"What kind of nonsense is that?" he said. But he held his blade steady.

She drew a single finger along the sword's edge, then pulled it away. "See? Blood."

Papa stared at this new ritual he'd never heard of—how could he when she'd fabricated it just now? Darsal felt her hand tremble as she reached for the book. It was going to work. *Please, Elyon, let this work . . .*

She lowered her bloody finger onto the leather cover. A hole large enough for any human to enter parted the air above her, buzzing with power. Darsal gasped. Her ears filled with the terrifying groan made by the dark, distorted figure beyond, who now beckoned her with his hand. She reached out. Touched the hole. Felt heat swim up her arm.

She was on her back, so she couldn't step in. But she didn't need to, because the gateway began to move toward her. Swallowing first her hand, then her arm. Darsal began to shake.

"Billos," she muttered.

The last thing she remembered was the sight of Karas diving through the air and grabbing her foot. Then her world went black.

eighteen

Billos considered the two guiding objectives of this mission that Marsuvees Black had sent him on: to practice his already crafted power and to find the books.

He stood with legs spread, understanding his situation perfectly. He'd strolled into the village of Paradise with a tentative grasp of his own skill, engaged the enemy, and overcome six of them with ridiculous ease.

But then, nothing less was expected of him—he was Billos of Southern, traveler of the books, wielder of the gun, born and bred to be master of all he put his hand to. This first test had been child's play.

The voices yelled outside, nearer now. This second attack wouldn't be nearly as easy.

To get the books first or to kill them, that was the question that stalled Billos perhaps a moment too long.

Books, he decided. The books harness a way of escape. But boots were already pounding on the steps just outside.

He dove to the base of the counter and rolled behind it. Scrambling like a crab over Steve's prone body, he snatched up the long gun with twin tubes that lay beside his slain prey.

The door crashed open. "Steve!"

Billos breathed steadily, measuring his time. The books sat on the shelf above him. He would rise, unload some suhupow into the man at the door, snatch the books, and make for the back door he could see just beyond the counter. Once outside, he would regroup and plot his attack on the rest of the village.

"Get Claude!" the voice cried. "We have a shooting here! Jerry's been shot! Call the station in Delta. Get the cops up here, for goodness' sake, hurry!"

Cops. The man had named Billos's enemy. "Imposters," Black had said. But he had yet to meet someone pretending to be someone else. His mission was far from over.

The man spoke low, aiming his verbal taunting at Billos now. "Listen to me, you—"

Billos rose while the man was full of his threat. He whipped the twin-tubed firing stick at the door and jerked both levers back.

Ba-boom!

Twin thunder crushed his ears. The device bucked like a stallion, slamming him backward into the wall behind him. Glasses and bottles rained to the floor, crashing around him. He'd misjudged the power of this new weapon.

The assailant, however, had misjudged Billos and now lay in a heap beyond the doors as payment for his lack of respect. "Dead by Billos," he said, then spun and reached high for the books.

Rolling thunder filled the room; the wall splintered near him.

He dropped to his knees. Reinforcements had reached the door and leveled a round of suhupow at him. He was lucky to be alive!

Okay then. Bring it to Billos; Billos will bring it to you. The books would have to wait.

"Steve!" They kept calling for Steve, which probably meant that Billos had taken out an important fellow. Maybe their commander.

"Steve's dead!" he yelled, snatching a second handgun off the shelf in favor over the larger stick. "As you and all your friends will be if you don't surrender." He dropped the big gun.

Suhupow thudded against the counter in response. Their arrogance was unforgivable!

He scooped up a jar and hurled it across the room. It crashed against the far wall, and the assailant instinctively shifted his fire in the same direction.

Billos rolled into the open, firing from both guns, flinging deadly fire toward a man who stood in the door. Behind him crouched three others, but their way was blocked by the staggering body of their fallen comrade.

Dead by Billos. The enemy had now seen him and knew what they were up against.

Billos launched himself at the rear door, flung it open, and ran into an alleyway behind the establishment. He flattened his back against the wall, guns cocked by his ears, panting. Unable to hold back a smirk of intense satisfaction.

Round one to Billos of Southern, baby. The sense of pride and power that swelled through him was unlike any he'd ever felt. It was almost as if he'd found his purpose, here in the histories. He'd been born for this.

But the sentiment was cut short the next moment, severed by the sight of four warriors who tore around the corner of the next building, scowling, armed with suhupow guns. The wood wall behind Billos splintered when the largest of the four whipped his gun up and leveled belching fire at him. This time Billos had no surprise in his favor, and the warriors had dispensed with the trickery that had made those inside seem so unthreatening.

What did it feel like to be struck with a gun's power? The question kept Billos momentarily fixed to the ground. His vision clouded, and he blinked. The forest behind the village distorted. A new kind of suhupow?

Billos's throat suddenly felt dry. His head spun. He pressed both hands on the wall behind him for balance, dropping the guns in the process.

Had he been killed? Was this what the gun's power felt like?

A voice whispered in his ears, low and mocking. "Is that all you have, Billos? Maybe you're not as smart as you think. You puke."

Then Billos's world turned white.

nineteen

I'm not saying that we aren't responsible, sir, only that I truly believe that we may be the only ones who can fix the situation."

Johnis stood next to Silvie, facing a furious commander who paced next to his wife, Rachelle, seated to his right. A single fluffy white Roush hopped along one of the rafter beams over Rachelle's head.

They were three personalities, each as distinct as the colors of Pampie fruit: Thomas the warrior, furious at those in his charge. Rachelle the lover, always ready to extend grace, though not at the expense of her wisdom. Hunter the Roush, who was desperate to make up for the embarrassment of allowing himself to be taken captive.

Thomas threw wide a dismissive hand. "Fix it? You caused it!

Every time I turn around, I find you four necks-deep in some quagmire of your own making! I simply can't believe you've lost not only Billos and Darsal but Karas of all people. What's her part in this? The next thing I know you'll have lost yourself."

"Well, sir, we think Karas might have been under the delusion that Darsal is her aunt," Johnis explained.

"Time's wasting!" the Roush cried, hopping along the rafter.

"Quiet!" Johnis snapped his frustration without thought, glancing up at the white bat.

"Pardon?" Thomas demanded.

Johnis realized his mistake immediately. Neither Thomas nor Rachelle could see the Roush, of course, and for the most part it was easy to hide the fact that he and Silvie could. However, it's not as easy when you're fighting and facing a hyperactive Roush who keeps insisting you have to leave. Even his superior, Michal, had agreed, he'd said.

Johnis closed his eyes and ground his molars. "Sorry, sir, I was only scolding myself." He walked to his right, scrambling for the right words. "You're right, we should be quiet. None of this makes sense to you, but it does to us. If you want us to become the kind of leaders who will lead our people in victory one day, you have to allow us to make our mistakes. Don't you think we're learning?"

"He's right, Thomas," Rachelle said quietly.

But Thomas was having none of it. "Mistakes, you say? And how many lives do you suggest I put in the way of your *mistakes*?"

"Point made," Silvie said. They would never forgive Johnis's indiscretion with the Third Fighting Group. As well they shouldn't.

Silvie faced Thomas. "Then let us leave alone, just the two of us. We'll take no army."

"To where?" he shouted. "Do you have some intelligence that I'm not aware of, because as I understand the situation, you don't know where they are."

"*I* know," the Roush said. "Just keep that in mind. I know exactly—"

"That's our problem," Johnis said to Thomas, this time keeping his eyes off the Roush.

"And you're my problem," Thomas said. "You're making me look like a fool. Don't forget that it was me who chose you."

"No, Thomas." Rachelle turned her head to her husband. "It wasn't you who chose him."

She was speaking of the circular birthmark on the side of his neck that marked him as Elyon's chosen one.

Thomas grunted. "Well, I'm beginning to wonder if Elyon's purpose in choosing this runt is to mortify me."

"He was a hero not two weeks ago," Rachelle said. "You don't remember the cheering?"

"And the next week he plotted to take my life! Yet here I am, giving him a secret audience in our chambers so that no one will hear that we're as foolish as he!"

"You do so because you know it's the right thing to do."

Thomas frowned, but he couldn't deny his wife's wisdom.

"Then you agree?" the Roush who'd called himself Hunter asked Thomas, knowing the man couldn't possibly hear him. "So be a leader and let them go before going makes no sense!"

"Karas could be invaluable to us," Thomas said, refusing to let the matter resolve easily.

"We were the ones who lost her," Johnis said. "You have to give us the opportunity to find her. I was the one who rescued her in the first place, for the love of Elyon! How can you deny me my right to go after her?"

"But you *are* holding something back," Rachelle said. "Aren't you, chosen one?"

How could he lie so directly to a woman who was his advocate? He couldn't. "I'm within my rights to hold back everything Elyon has told me," Johnis said, then added so as to sound more like a chosen one, "All in good time."

Thomas lowered himself into a chair next to Rachelle, crossed his legs, folded his hands over one knee, and looked at Johnis. For a few long moments he just stared at him.

"Fine," he finally said. "I'll give you my permission—for my wife's sake—to go after them, but on the condition that you tell me everything when this is over."

"Everything?"

"You can't do it," the Roush said.

Johnis glanced up at him, and this time Rachelle followed his eyes and saw nothing but an empty rafter.

Her eyes lowered and met his. *What do you see, chosen one?* But he couldn't know what she was thinking.

"What if Elyon forbids my telling you everything?"

"Elyon has put you under my authority, and I say tell me. So then Elyon has spoken, through me. Do you think I'm not his servant as well?"

The commander had a point. He'd have to sort it all out later.

"Okay, I'll tell you everything," Johnis said.

Then he swept his hand toward the door. "Don't let me hold you back. Find them. Bring them back. Alive. And don't forget your vow."

"What vow?"

"You already forget?"

"To tell you everything. It's a vow?"

"Your word to your commander is, by extension of your commission, all vow. Are you having second thoughts?"

"No. No, just looking for clarity."

"Not good," the Roush said.

Thomas lowered his arm. "Elyon knows that you could use some clarity. Now move. The sun doesn't stop, even for the chosen one."

Rachelle reached out and touched her husband's knee, smiling. She winked. "Have I told you that my blood boils when I look at you?"

"I make you angry?" he asked with a glint in his eyes.

She just winked.

"Go, go!" the Roush quipped, fluttering his wings. "Water and swords. Lots of water!"

"I hope you're right about this," Thomas said to Rachelle as Johnis and Silvie slid from the room.

"Have I ever been wrong?"

But Johnis knew that there was always a first time for everything.

The blackness that swallowed Darsal when she entered the book felt like her imaginations of death, swirling and turning toward a bottomless chasm lined with charred trees and black Shataiki.

But then white light flooded her eyes, and she saw a bottom, rushing up. She crashed onto a hard surface with a loud grunt that echoed in her ears.

It took a moment for her head to clear. She pushed herself to one knee, scanned the square room, and froze solid. She was in what appeared to be a white room, at the center of which sat a lone monster, the likes of which had never crossed her imagination, much less her sight.

"What is it?"

Darsal jerked her eyes from the beast and twisted to see Karas up on one arm, staring past her.

And behind Karas . . . behind Karas the Scab, Papa, crouched, hand on his sword, staring at the beast. Two thoughts rushed through Darsal's mind: The first was that both Karas and Papa had followed her to hell or wherever this was, perhaps because they had been in contact with her when she'd touched the book with her blood. The second was that she never could have imagined feeling so relieved to have an armed Scab by her side.

She jumped to her feet and spun her eyes back over the beast. It was then that she saw Billos. Strapped onto one of the six legs, like a fly caught in a spider's web. His head was enshrouded in a black cocoon. Hands inserted in gloves.

Karas's thin voice came again. "Is he dead?"

Darsal stepped warily to her right, ready to jump back if the thing moved. Billos's chest rose and fell rapidly, she now saw. But she had no doubt that the black cocoon around his head would suffocate him if she didn't free him immediately.

She pushed aside caution for her own safety and moved closer.

"Stay back!" Papa rasped. "What foul beast is this?"

Darsal reached her hand back. "Give me your knife!"

His grasp on his sword didn't budge. He would be ready to swing at any appendage that might swipe his way.

"I'm not going to come after you, you oaf," Darsal snapped. "We have bigger problems now. Give me a blade!"

Papa slipped a long curved knife from his waist and tossed it toward her. She snatched it out of the air.

"Be careful," Karas said. "Please, Darsal, you're going to get us killed."

"You're assuming we aren't already dead."

The thing hadn't moved its legs. A flat, glassy panel against the wall showed several green and yellow lines moving across from left to right. Red eyes glared around a softly humming head with the word DELL written in block letters on one side. It was clearly alive, but nothing on its body had actually moved.

Then again, spiders sat in perfect stillness, waiting for their prey to come in close before leaping forward to sting them with poison. She would have to be careful.

"Can I have your sword?" she asked Papa without turning.

"Don't push it."

"I'm better with it than you are. Faster at least."

"As I recall, my blade was at your throat when you touched the book."

"There were four of you!" she said.

"There was only one of me."

It was hopeless. "Then get up here beside me and cover my flank."

Papa wasn't the type to show his fear. He stepped up, sword ready.

"Darsal . . ." Karas hung back. "Please, Darsal . . ."

"If it moves," Darsal whispered, "hack at the leg holding

Billos. Cut the veins." She nodded at the black ropes that ran along the hardened structure.

"Ready?"

The Scab shifted. "Ready."

Darsal held the Horde knife in her right hand and inched forward. She dove at Billos when she was within three feet, taking full advantage of the same kind of speed that the Forest Guard relied on to defeat the Horde.

With a flip of her wrist she sliced the gloves that gripped her man's hands. Still no movement. She grabbed the cocoon over his head with both hands and pulled hard, thinking at the last moment that it looked more like a strange helmet than a cocoon. It came off with surprising ease.

Billos lay still, his white face beaded with sweat, breathing hard. His eyes were wide and staring into the middle distance.

Darsal's first thought was that he had been paralyzed by this beast. But then he blinked and sat up, and she knew she'd freed him. Still concerned about a counterattack, she grabbed his arm and tugged hard, hauling him off the seatlike leg. Still dazed, Billos slid off and fell to the ground like a log. He grunted.

"What? What?"

"Hurry, Billos! Help me, Papa." With the Scab's help she dragged him away across the floor to where Karas stood watching.

"Stop it!" Billos's arms flailed, and he rolled to his feet. He stood and stared at them, clearly disoriented.

"I'm not sure he liked that," Karas said.

"Darsal? What's going on?"

She glanced at the spider thing and saw that its eyes had darkened. Still no movement.

"I don't know, Billos. You tell me."

"You . . . Where's the village?" He patted his chest and felt his head. "I'm okay?"

"No blood, if that's what you mean." But she couldn't say that he was okay, because his mind may have been compromised. He certainly didn't seem too eager to see her.

"How did I get back in here?" he demanded angrily.

"Settle down. It was you who caused this. I just followed with another book."

"I was here when you found me?"

"Are you daft, boy?" Papa said. "She said you were."

Billos was too preoccupied to give the Scab a second look. He crossed to the leg she'd freed him from and lifted the helmet.

"How did you find me?"

"I told you, the spider—"

"It's a contraption, not an animal," he snapped. "I couldn't figure out how it worked so I . . ."

He ran to the only door leading from the room and tugged on the handle. But it would not so much as budge.

"I got out," Billos said.

"Well, you weren't out just now," Papa said. "Don't tell me you don't know where we are or how we escape."

Billos faced the Desert Dweller. "Who let this thug in?"

"Your cursed book," Papa said. "Where are we?"

"Still in the white room, clearly." He glanced around. "I left this place; walked out that door; met a 'Marsuvees Black,' who gave me a gun; went to battle in the village of Paradise, where I clearly had the upper hand when . . ." Billos looked at Darsal. "Are we dead?"

It was a good question, but she was amazed that Billos didn't seem to be giving her a second thought.

"I risked my life to follow you," she said. "Please don't tell me all I've managed to do is follow you into death."

He looked at the spider contraption. "You're suggesting that I never left this room. Or that I left it and was returned with the magical power. Like the gun."

"What's this 'gun' business?" Papa demanded.

"A magical weapon that destroys objects from afar. You said you came with a book?"

"Yes," Darsal said.

"Then I know where it is. It's in Paradise, the village Marsuvees Black sent me to."

Darsal's mind was having difficulty keeping up with all of his disjointed comments. They seemed to be alive, which was a good thing. But they also seemed to be trapped in some kind of white prison.

"How do we get back?"

"To Paradise?" Billos asked.

"To Middle. To Thomas and Silvie and Johnis!"

He blinked. "With the books, I suppose. Not that we should go back, mind you. This is bigger than Johnis."

"We're trapped in this box with a contraption that you don't know how to work. Doesn't look so big to me."

He stared at her. "You're going to have to learn to trust me now. Once and for all."

"Is that so? The one who broke all the rules and ran off with the books? Which, I might add, are now lost. Why should I trust you?"

"Because I have the suhupow. I'm the chosen one."

She frowned, upset at finding him with this attitude after he'd put her through so much.

"You abandoned her," Karas said. "A little sensitivity would be helpful about now."

Billos could have refuted the girl. Instead he glanced at her, softened, and approached Darsal. "I'm sorry. I had to know. But it's worked out. I would have come back for you."

His words, however sketchy, filled her with warmth. She knew his heart.

"Would you? You don't have the books. We're trapped. You don't even know how to make this contraption work."

Billos smiled and touched her cheek tenderly. "Oh? Maybe that's where you're wrong."

She couldn't help but lean into him. Billos wrapped his arms around her. It was all she could do to keep her tears back. "I was so afraid," she whispered into his musky neck.

"I'm sorry; I didn't mean to leave you."

"Never again, Billos."

"I swear. Never again."

They stood in the embrace for a few seconds while she regained her composure.

"Nice, but I'm feeling no less trapped," Papa said.

Darsal pulled back. "Okay, tell me everything."

twenty-one

Billos finished his tale and left them all staring at him incredulously. Papa was the first to speak.

"This is the most preposterous thing a man can stand to hear," he mumbled. Then louder, glaring at Billos, "You're saying that you found these books in the Black Forest under our noses? That we are blind to both the Black Forest and the books, not to mention Shataiki and Roush?"

"It's true," Karas said. "My eyes were opened as well. I saw Shataiki, I saw the Roush, and I saw the Black Forest."

"Even so, how do you know this isn't all just trickery in the mind? You say you went into the blasted village named Paradise without ever leaving this place. How do you know you ever left Middle Forest to begin with? For all we know we're still in the desert at this moment. The books are probably only making us believe we're in this white room!"

"Impossible," Darsal corrected him. "I saw Billos vanish into the books."

"Well, forgive my smallest doubt." Papa made a tiny sign between his thumb and forefinger. "Billos also believed he was in the so-called 'village of Paradise' when we saw him lying right here."

"Your mind's clogged," Karas said. "Your judgment is the least trustworthy here. I should know; I was Scab only a few days ago."

"Is that so, supposed daughter of Witch? And I should listen to a child?"

"I had the good sense to bathe in their water. Do you?"

"And now you smell like they do."

"Stop this!" Darsal snapped. To Billos: "What now?"

He tapped his fingers together and walked around the contraption. "The best I can figure, I escaped this place by donning the helmet and the gloves and speaking the right commands, not unlike a horse."

"But you didn't leave this place," Papa said. "If I'm the diseased one, why is this fact only obvious to me?"

"Because it's not that simple, Papa," Karas said. "Even if he did leave it only in his mind, he found three books there. The one we brought is probably there as well now. They're the key to our escape."

Papa waved his hand at Billos. "This fool talks as if he doesn't even want to escape! All this talk of guns and Marcudeves—"

"Marsuvees," Billos corrected.

"Whatever. Some demon who ordered you to slay common village folk."

"The enemy, armed with guns."

"Which you say they only used in defense," Papa pointed out.

"They had the books!" He gripped his head. "Why are we listening to this slug of diseased flesh? You should have killed him in the desert."

"Fine, kill me when you get your hands on one of these magical guns of yours. Until then, don't think this sword won't put you on your backside."

Billos humphed.

"Will you all stop arguing like spoiled children?" Darsal demanded.

"Yeah," Karas chimed in. "Grow up, both of you."

They all glanced at her.

Darsal walked up to the contraption and ran her hand over one of the helmets she'd mistaken for a cocoon spun from black thread. "Billos is right about the books. We need them to return. Even if there was a way to return without them, we wouldn't dare. If we return with all four books, on the other hand, all might be forgiven."

She faced Billos. "So we follow the books. As long as we agree to return the moment we find them. We're not staying in this lost Paradise of yours, no matter where it is. We have an obligation to Johnis."

Billos nodded slowly, but he didn't look convinced. "Fine."

"He doesn't mean it," Karas said.

"Shut your hole!" Billos snapped. "We should leave you as well."

Darsal felt defensive of the girl, a sentiment that surprised her some. "Easy, Billos. She's my sister. Niece, to be more precise, but she likes to call me her sister."

"Your niece? She's a Scab."

"And not long ago the Scabs and we were one," Karas said. "Or did you forget your history lessons?"

He looked from one to the other, then turned away. "Bring your niece, if that's who she really is, and bring your Scab dog; what do I care? Just keep them out of my way."

He slid up onto the same chair Darsal had rescued him from.

"So we put on the helmets and the gloves?" Darsal asked, touching another chair. "Then what?"

"Then you speak a command. 'Let's go, you haggard beast.'"

"This contraption responds to being called a haggard beast?" Papa asked, warily approaching another seat.

"Shut up and lie down." Billos grinned, then added, "Baby."

"Baby?" Papa glared. "You think I respond to insults?"

"You're acting crazy, Billos," Darsal said. "We're all under considerable stress; go easy!"

"Yes, sir. Baby."

"Why do you call us that?"

He shrugged, then pulled on his helmet. Slipped on his gloves. Spoke into the cocoon over his head. "Let's go, you haggard beast."

The contraption named DELL began to hum, and the red lights

around its crown brightened. The flat glass panel on the wall flickered and showed several lines.

Billos's body immediately arched, then slowly relaxed.

Darsal glanced at Karas, who'd climbed into a seat, then at Papa. "Seems to have worked."

"He's still here," Papa said.

"Do you have a better idea?"

The Scab grunted and pulled on his helmet.

Darsal's world went dark inside the musty-smelling headpiece. She slipped her hands into the gloves on either side, pried her eyes for a view of something besides darkness, and, seeing nothing, spoke aloud.

"Let's go, you haggard beast."

Nothing happened that she could tell. Maybe her helmet was ruined. She tried again. "Let's go, you haggard beast!"

Still nothing.

Darsal finally sat up, pulled her helmet off, and turned to the others. "What's supposed . . ."

The others were gone. Darsal faced five empty seats. Alarmed, she scanned the room, but there was no sign of them. They'd made it out and left her?

The door . . .

She flew off the seat and had crossed halfway to the door before realizing that it was ajar. She reached for the knob, threw it wide, and stared out to a dusty alley bordered by a green forest.

"Billos?"

Wind kicked up a dust devil and sent it scurrying down the alley. Darsal stepped out and looked one way, then the other.

"Billos!"

The wind slammed the door shut behind her, and she jumped.

Muffled voices reached her from down the alleyway. It took her only a moment to realize that an angry mob was prowling the streets out of her direct line of sight.

"You see them, you kill them on sight!" a voice shouted. "Spread out!"

The villagers are responding to Billos's assault, she thought. And if she was right, she was one of *them* the villagers were after. She had to get out of sight.

"In here!"

Darsal spun to the sound of Karas's voice. The young girl stood in the same doorway through which Darsal had exited the white room. But the space behind Karas wasn't white.

She leapt past the girl into a room with numerous shelves, each filled with supplies. Small containers made of metal and colored bags unlike any she'd ever seen. To her left stood a large cabinet made of silver with glass doors, behind which sat white containers that read MILK. The sign over the counter on her right indicated that this was a store named ALL RIGHT CONVENIENCE.

Behind the counter stood Billos, dressed in a full-length black coat and broad-rimmed black hat. He was looking down the tube of a strange contraption, something like the gun he'd described. Several similar guns rested on the counter in front of him.

Billos looked up as Karas shut the door. "Nice of you to join us." He tossed the weapon at Darsal, who caught it out of the air. "Same gun I used to teach them a lesson the first time," he said with a smirk.

"What are we doing, Billos? There's a mob headed this way!"

"Battle, baby. Point and shoot." He snatched another gun from the mantel behind him. "We're going to kill them."

"Kill who?" Karas asked.

Billos lobbed a gun at her, and she caught it clumsily.

"Kill them all," he said.

twenty-two

T his isn't good," Johnis said, staring at the dead Scabs among the boulders. "They've been tagged."

"And it's clear that they were killed by Guard."

Rather than taking the time to bury their dead, the Horde sometimes—only when it was convenient—tagged the corpses with black feathers taken from the Dambu crow to speed their delivery into the afterlife. The fact that they were tagged meant they'd been found by the Horde.

The fact that Darsal's knife was still buried in one of their necks meant that whoever had found them knew they'd been killed by members of the Forest Guard.

"This is way out of our territory," Silvie said. "They won't let it go."

Johnis scanned the horizon. "Hopefully they'll just send a scouting party. How far did you say?"

The Roush flapped to steady himself on one of the boulders. "Just past the rise. But they made it out. This killing was done after I left them."

"Do you see any tracks heading south from here?" Johnis asked.

"None. They head only in the direction of this Black Forest no one has seen. They don't see me either," Hunter said. "Does that mean I'm not real?"

Johnis wheeled his horse around and headed into the desert, north. Hunter landed between the animal's ears and repeated the same lecture he'd offered a dozen times in the last day.

"Remember—water, you have to use the water. The Shataiki are terrified of the water. And I can't go. Not alone. They'll rip my wings off and feed them to their young. We can't have any young Shataiki growing up with Roush in their bellies."

"So we've heard," Johnis said. "Isn't that them?" He nodded at the horizon.

"Where?" Hunter whirled around, saw the same black bat sitting as a mere dot on the rise ahead, and began to bounce on the horse's head. "Okay, okay. That's them, that's them."

Silvie rode stoically by Johnis's side, eyes fixed forward. Her wind-tossed tangles hung in messy but perfect symmetry. Fine features darkened by the sun betrayed her femininity, but a single glance at her ripped shoulders and you would know that this one had been born with a sword in her hands. She could easily put most men on the ground in a number of ways.

She felt Johnis's stare and looked into his eyes. He reached out his hand and took hers. Any ordinary sixteen-year-old girl facing the prospect of Teeleh's lair, as she had only a couple weeks ago, might have reacted with the same reluctance that she had then.

But Silvie was no ordinary girl. The last few weeks had re-shaped her.

She winked at him, then faced forward again.

"Okay, okay, I'll wait by the rocks. Maybe this isn't such a good idea. Maybe Thomas is right."

"Maybe," Johnis said. "We have water. We'll be okay."

"Don't think they don't learn. You lose the water and you're dead meat, as Thomas likes to say." Hunter hopped once, twice. "Okay . . ." He flapped into the air. "Remember the plan. Every detail. You have to get them back. Okay . . ."

Hunter soared low to pick up speed, then flapped south, toward the boulders where he would keep watch as long as he could, as planned.

"What details?" Silvie asked.

"Exactly." They had no details. This was entirely "ride where the horse takes you." But Hunter seemed to find comfort in having contributed to a plan, which was really no more than *Find them; get them out; water, water, water.*

Lines of black bats seemed to rise from the hazy desert as they crested the rise. Johnis pulled up. Ahead lay the hidden Black

Forest, gouged from the ground by some unseen claw. It went underground, Hunter said. Abruptly, by the looks of it, not two hundred meters ahead.

Johnis felt a shiver run down his spine despite the afternoon heat. This was the second Black Forest they'd encountered. Hunter didn't know how many there were, probably hundreds if you went far enough. All hidden from ordinary eyes.

Yet it had been here all along. Johnis wondered what would happen if a horse happened upon it. Would it fall in or walk over it as if it didn't exist? He'd have to ask the Roush.

"You ready for this?" Silvie asked.

"No. You?"

"Not really. But that's never stopped us before."

He nodded. "Douse yourself in water."

They both withdrew leather bags filled with lake water and splashed it on their faces and chests. They would keep the bags as their only weapon from here in.

"We go for the lair under the lake," Johnis said. "Let the horse have its head once we're in. Besides the water, we have only speed."

"This lair that not even Hunter can confirm," Silvie said.

"I was in Teeleh's lair and felt his presence. I assure you, each forest has a lair."

She knew that he could not be so sure, but that, too, had never stopped them.

"Then let's go," Silvie said, and kicked her horse.

twenty-three

Billos wanted one thing and one thing only. To kill as many of these crafty, double-crossing villagers as he could turn his suhupow gun on.

It had occurred to him back in the white room that he was just a bit put out with Darsal for dragging the Scab she called Papa and the little piece of trash, Karas, into his world. In fact, he was bothered that she herself had managed to find him. He found it all oddly threatening.

And he found the way she was looking at him now even more threatening.

"Kill them all? We can't just start killing these people," Darsal said.

"Oh yes, we can. And if we don't, they'll kill us. Think of them as the Horde. Kill them all: those are our orders."

"The orders of a man we've never met," Papa said. "Who may be Teeleh for all we know."

"No one asked for your opinion, Scab. Doesn't the Horde worship Teeleh?"

Billos hurried to the front window and peeked past a drawn drape. Two uniformed warriors with silver badges on their chests were climbing out of a black-and-white buggy topped with flashing lights.

The establishment in which Billos had dispatched Steve and his jukebox warriors was only a stone's toss from here.

"Billos?"

He spun to Darsal, who was watching him with wide eyes. "What?" he snapped.

"What's happening?"

"Are you deaf? I told you what's happening! I suggest you snap out of it and make yourself useful."

"Is that what I mean to you? Just a tool to dispatch for your own purposes?"

"What are you talking about? We're in a battle. Are you blind as well?"

Her eyes glared. He'd seen this look of defiance a thousand times, and he knew that his words would do nothing to win her over.

"I'm talking about the way you look at me, as if my coming to save you means nothing. All you want to do is kill villagers. From the moment you climbed out of that chair in the white room, you've had nothing on your mind but flexing this new power of yours."

She was being about as logical as a stick of firewood. "I'm trying to save *you*!" retorted Billos.

"Is now really the time for this?" Papa asked, parting the shade next to the rear exit. Several warriors ran past the window in the direction of the establishment where Billos had slain Steve.

"Save me?" Darsal whispered harshly. "It's always me, the poor little girl who's being beaten by her uncle, that needs saving, is that it?"

"Are you saying I shouldn't have saved you back then? You'd be dead now."

"Maybe you shouldn't have. Not if you intended to make me your slave instead!"

After Darsal's parents had been killed when she was only eight, her uncle, Blaken the Blacksmith, who was too much of a coward to fight with the Guard but had proven his value by crafting metal swords, had taken her in. He used to beat her in drunken fits, but Darsal was too shy to confess her plight to anyone. Billos had witnessed such a beating late one night when he was out sneaking through the streets of Southern, looking for trouble. He had taken it upon himself to break into her room and introduce himself.

When the beatings had become unbearable six months later, Billos had arranged an accident that had put Blaken on crutches. Permanently.

"How did you suddenly become my slave?" he demanded,

flummoxed by her strained connections. "I'm trying to save us here, for the sake of Elyon!"

"No, I don't think so. I think you're trying to save your own neck for the sake of *Billos*. That's the way you've always been. It's always about Billos, isn't it?"

"I think my sister is right," Karas said.

Billos looked at the young converted Horde and suppressed the flashing impulse to level his gun at her. Why was he so bothered by these three intruders?

"And I think you're both going to get us all killed," he snapped. "This is complete nonsense! If you can't do what needs to be done, then leave."

Darsal stared at him for a moment longer, then set her jaw and averted her eyes. "Where are the books?"

Something clicked deep inside of Billos's mind with those words. Something that sounded as much like Marsuvees Black as him. *The books, Billos, she's here for the books.*

At first he didn't fully understand the significance of this suggestion, because it seemed a bit obvious. Then another thought whispered through his head. *She'll take the books and leave you powerless.* And he knew she would, to protect him, she would say.

You know what that makes her, don't you Billy-babe? His mind remained blank. *A traitor who will end up cutting you off at the knees and shoving her heel in your face.*

Darsal shoved her gun under her tunic and strode for the door. She grabbed the handle and pulled it open.

"What are you doing?" Billos demanded. "You'll give us away!"

She stood in the open doorway and drilled him with a glare. "Will I? They don't know me as a threat. Unlike you, I haven't killed here."

"You're dressed like a complete stranger."

"Then they'll find me a curiosity, not a threat. Now, tell me where you saw the books."

"Get back inside!" he snapped, waving his gun in her direction.

Instead she took a step outside. "An eating establishment, you said?" She looked up and down the street, then settled on a building to her right. "On the shelf above the counter. Shouldn't be hard." Back to him: "I suggest you toss the black Shataiki getup and follow me."

"She makes sense," Papa said, crossing to the front door.

"Are you mad? If Darsal looks like a complete stranger to them, you look like a monster with your diseased skin!"

"Don't be a fool," Papa shot back gruffly. "You're assuming this place has no Horde. The Horde probably rule here!"

"I didn't see any."

"Because this is a diseased village that—"

"Shut up!" Karas was following as well.

Billos waved his gun again. "Get inside, all of you."

"Or?" Darsal challenged.

"Or you'll shoot my sister, whom you supposedly love?" Karas demanded.

"I might choose you instead. Or the monster."

"No, you won't," Papa said, spitting to one side.

"Don't presume to know the way things work in this new place. All bets are off. I'd pray for the chance to kill you in the desert. Maybe Elyon would answer that prayer here, in Paradise."

"Then Paradise would be your fall," Darsal said. "You said that the suhupow makes a loud boom when it kills. This enemy of yours would come running like rats to the hole. Has this DELL-god robbed your mind as well as your heart?"

Then she walked into the street, followed promptly by Papa and Karas.

Billos stood in the All Right Convenience store dressed in black, holding his gun and at a complete loss as to what he should do.

So he began to swear bitterly under his breath.

twenty-four

Darsal may have never walked out into the village had she not been so perturbed with Billos. But these past few days, spent slogging through the desert on a desperate mission to save his skinny neck after he'd abandoned her, had robbed her of the grace she'd offered him for years. His dismissal of her raked on her nerves like a saw.

She marched along the sidewalk toward the building called Smither's Barbeque. Two men in strange blue costumes were entering, holding their guns up near their heads. She briefly wondered if the weapons also doubled as listening devices.

"You're just going to walk in?" Papa asked.

"Now you're afraid of being Horde?" She glanced back at the large man with flaking white skin. His leather armor, which wasn't so different from her own, might prevent their blending as much as his skin.

"I told you, you should have bathed," Karas said.

Papa grunted.

Ahead of them, the outer screened door to the eatery banged shut on its own. Two coils of wire seemed to be responsible for the closing. Darsal scanned the rest of the village. The buildings themselves were square and not so unusual looking, but the buggies were made of many colors of metal. No horses that she could see.

Tall metal poles with glass hoods perched atop; smooth black rock laid down as the main road; glass windows everywhere; strange costumes such as those worn by the two warriors who'd entered the eatery—these were the stuff of suhupow that had swept Billos off his feet and made him so power hungry.

"Keep your weapons covered," Darsal said, mounting the steps.

"How do I hide the sword?"

"Toss it. Karas, give your gun to Papa. But hide it. We want no fight."

She pushed the door open and stepped in, intending to show no concern. But the scene inside stopped her cold. One of the blue costumed warriors lay unmoving on her left, and three other bodies had been arranged side by side just beyond. Billos's little war in the eatery had left its mark.

"Hold up!"

She looked up at a warrior who was pointing a gun at her. One of the two who'd just entered. He spoke quickly into a small black box in his left hand.

"Come back, Pete; how'd you say the perp was dressed?"

The box spoke back. "Black trench coat," it said.

Karas spoke the wonder on all their minds. "Is that suhupow?"

Darsal knew it had to be. Surely no man was small enough, no matter what world, to fit into such a small box. The two warriors seemed as stunned by them as they were by the talking box. They fixed their eyes on Papa.

"No quick moves," the one said.

Darsal lifted her hands to set him at ease. "We mean no harm."

"What's with him?" the warrior asked, nodding at Papa. "Are you contagious, buddy?"

"Papa," the Scab said. "My name is Papa, not Buddy."

"Yes," Karas said. "Papa is contagious."

The man immediately lifted a hand to shield his mouth and nose. "I'm going to have to ask you to leave."

"Nonsense!" Papa boomed. "She's only making trouble. Depending on how you look at it, one of us has a skin condition, and for the sake of argument I'll accept the role. But it can't spread!"

"Then how did you get it?" Karas pushed.

Darsal glanced at the young girl. "Karas, please."

"I've always had it," Papa said.

"You turned into a Scab when evil was released from the Forbidden Circle. If you bathed in one of the lakes, you might know that."

It occurred to Darsal that crafty prodding by Karas might play to their advantage. She scanned the shelf above the counter.

On it sat four Books of History, exactly as Billos said he'd seen the three. Clearly the books ended up here when one entered them. And if he was right, only they could see them. Their way back to the forests waited for them.

Then again, these four books could also take anyone to Earth, the Earth that Alucard had traded his book for, wherever that was.

It was strange to think that at this very moment they were neither in the desert reality nor in this reality called Earth, but trapped somewhere between. In the cover. "In the skin of the worlds," as Alucard had said.

Darsal shivered. *You've made a mistake, girl. A very bad mistake that will haunt more than you.*

"Forgive them," she said to the first warrior who—evidently concluding that he was faced with imbeciles rather than killers—lowered his gun. "Karas is right. Papa is diseased, as you can clearly see. It affects his mind as well as his flesh. The physician sent us here for four books, one of which contains the cure to his disease. He said they'd be on the shelf behind the counter."

The warrior followed her glance to what he perceived was an empty shelf, then regarded her evenly. "Books, eh? Even so, this isn't exactly a clinic. What would medical books be doing here?"

"Not medical books. Books of History that mention this uncommon disease."

"Disease called what?"

"Called Teeleh," Karas said.

Darsal nodded. "Teeleh."

"And what's with the armor?" the second warrior asked, speaking for the first time.

"It protects us," Karas offered.

"Then why aren't you wearing any?"

"Teeleh is more effective in grown-ups."

The warrior seemed to be judging her words carefully. "What's the name of this physician?"

"Why do you ask so many questions?" Karas wanted to know.

"Because I think you're hiding something. Give me the name of the physician, and we'll check out your story."

"His name is Thomas of Hunter," Karas said, as if she had no doubt in the matter.

He lifted the black box and spoke into it again. "Pete, track down a doctor named Thomas Hunter and get back to me as soon as you've located him."

Darsal knew that they'd bought some time, but none of this would help them when they found no physician named Hunter.

"Without the armor, you're likely to be infected by now," Karas said.

"You really expect me to believe any of this?"

The girl shrugged. "Then you, too, can look like Papa. And smell like him. Like rotten eggs."

The man swallowed, eyes on Papa.

"At least let us look at the books," Darsal said.

"What books?"

Darsal stepped forward. "I'll show you."

"Easy now!"

"You want to see the books, I'll show you. If I go for anything but the books, feel free to level fire at me. Fair?"

He didn't answer, which she took as encouragement enough to slip past the counter and reach for the four books. In her hands they appeared perfectly natural; it struck her as odd that the warrior couldn't see them.

She faced him, four books tight between her two palms.

He looked from her hands to her eyes, lost momentarily in that gaze that clearly expressed pity for one's foolishness. She had to get one book to each of the others without interference from the warriors. Better now, quickly, before he grew difficult.

"You don't see them?" she demanded, stepping forward.

"Stop."

She stopped.

He pressed the lever on the side of the box and issued an order. "Never mind that last order, Pete. Bring the car around. I have three suspects I want you to put in custody."

"Copy that. No listing of a Hunter here anyway."

The warrior nodded and lifted his gun again. "Any of you happen to be carrying a nine-millimeter pistol?"

Darsal nonchalantly slid the books under the counter in full view of the officer. He undoubtedly saw only her setting nothing on the shelf. And when the time was right, he would see all three of them picking nothing up off the shelf before vanishing.

But first this annoyance at explaining that they had nothing to do with the slain warriors on the floor.

"Hands up where I can see them!" the man snapped.

Darsal lifted both arms.

twenty-five

Billos stood in the storeroom alone, fighting a terrible volley of conflicting emotions. On the one hand, he knew that Darsal was right to level her glares at him. He was the one who'd gotten them into this fix in the first place.

He'd broken ranks and abandoned her, knowing deep inside that she would follow because she was as loyal as a puppy dog—had been ever since he rescued her. And he had been as loyal to her.

But he couldn't deny the fact that he hated the way she was acting now. From the moment she'd stuck her head into his business here, liking her had been a challenge. Something was wrong with her.

Or with you, Billos.

Nonsense.

Still, he knew that he'd changed a little since becoming aware of the power at his fingertips. Marsuvees Black was both intoxicating and disturbing, as was all true power. Darsal stood in the way of that power. The question was whether her doing so was a good thing or a bad thing.

A low voice spoke on his left. "They're going to string you up like a straw doll."

Billos whipped his gun around and faced Marsuvees Black, who leaned against the rear wall. The black-clad man was grinning, picking his teeth with a tiny spike of wood. His big hands looked as if they could crush a face like a tomato.

Billos found his voice. "What?"

"You started out well, my man. Put four of them on their backs and returned to finish it all—not bad for a scrapper from the past."

"Six," Billos said. "The two with the sticks and balls . . ."

"That's a pool table."

"One behind the counter."

"And the counter is a bar."

"One warrior at the door."

"A cop," Black said.

"And the two singers."

Black hesitated. "That's a jukebox. It runs on electricity, not blood. Doesn't count."

"All with suhupow," Billos said.

"Bullets, my man. The gun shoots bullets." Black straightened. "The point is you got a handful, and that's just fine. But there are a couple hundred more, and I want you to kill every single one of them. Like Joshua in the battle of Jericho. Don't leave a single one of them breathing. You hearing me?"

Now it was Billos's turn to hesitate. "Yes."

"Well, you don't sound or look *Yes* to me. You look a bit like a ghost in a black costume."

Black was insulting him. Anger flared up Billos's neck. What was to say he couldn't tilt up the suhupow gun and put this thug on his back right now?

The man's hand blurred. He transformed in the blink of an eye from casual observer to warrior, clutching a gun he'd snatched off his hip. His lips twisted with each word.

"I don't think you understand who you're dealing with, sugar lips."

Another insult, no doubt. But Billos had to admit, Black would prove to be a monstrous adversary. Best to deal with his kind in kind.

"Did I threaten you, you black slug?"

A smile pulled at the edges of Black's mouth. He spun the weapon in his hand as if it were a toy, then slammed it home in the scabbard on his hip. He withdrew his hand and cracked his knuckles.

"Can I have one of those?" Billos asked.

"Slap your hip, baby. The holster will be there."

The suhupow Black brought with him was enough to make Billos's head spin. He impulsively spun his gun, poorly mimicking the man's move, and shoved it down against his hip. The gun slapped into a holster.

Billos withdrew his hand and cracked his knuckles.

"Just a tad juvenile, don't you think? I know how good it feels. Trust me, the feelings that come with true power will make your knees tremble. I can make your wildest fantasy real."

It occurred to Billos that the slight tremble now in his fingers was the result of desire. He'd never felt it so strongly.

"Or I can cut you to ribbons and feed you to the crows. Which, to be perfectly honest, happens to be *my* wildest fantasy."

"Assuming you could," Billos said, only slightly alarmed.

"And that's why I chose you."

"What is?"

"The fact that you're so full of yourself that you actually believe I won't ruin you for life. Takes a strong fool to knowingly play with me. A king. The chosen one. You, baby."

Billos wasn't sure how to take these backhanded compliments. But he did know that his fingers were still trembling.

"Are you ready to hunt?" Black asked.

The village outside had gone strangely quiet. "I was born ready."

"Then get me the books. And kill them all."

"Stop talking my ear off and I will."

"And to make up for your stupidity, I want you to bring me the imposters, Dorksel included. Share the spoils."

"How do you know they're imposters?"

He ignored the question. "Kill the big creep; bring me the two pop tarts."

Billos stared at the door. He could feel, maybe hear, a bead of sweat breaking past his temple.

"It's all about the books, baby," Black said softly. "You know she's an imposter, because she'll come between you and the books. So you choose between the power of the books and this one imposter who may mean something now but will mean nothing when you're on top. Think of it as your sacrifice, the only one I'm asking you to make for me."

The tremble in Billos's fingers was now motivated by something more than desire. Destiny and fear, all mixed into one heady, powerful emotion.

"You choose between yourself and her. Give me one or the other. The crows are waiting."

What choice did he have? Even the Roush had commanded him to retrieve the books. Well, he'd found them, hadn't he? And now Darsal was standing in his way. On the other hand, even though he didn't feel it now, he cared for Darsal. More than he'd ever admitted to her.

"Fine," Billos said. But when he turned back to face the man with his decision, Black was gone.

Billos stood still for a moment, then stripped off the black coat and hat. He withdrew his gun, cocked it up by his ear, and strode for the door.

Time to hunt.

twenty-six

Johnis plunged into the Black Forest, gripping the horse with his knees so that both hands remained free for his water bag, his left clenching the leather seam, his right shoved into the water for the teaming Shataiki above to clearly see. Silvie's horse pounded the narrow forest trail behind him.

Without so much as a word, they'd approached the precipice that fell into the hole and headed down a path cut from the cliff. Throngs of the beasts circled and squawked on all sides, keeping just beyond the reach of any water flung their way. At the top Johnis had knocked two of them from midair with a single flick of his wet fingers. Clearly, fire wasn't the beasts' only fear; the lake water was poison to their skin—even a tiny spot of mist would kill one of these vampires. Had they known this several weeks ago, their task might have been simpler.

Still, the Shataiki dove in as close as they dared, desperate to catch one of them unaware.

"Watch your back!" Silvie cried behind him.

Johnis spun as a mangy bat veered into the thick jungle and slammed into a trunk. It fell in a heap. Killed by Silvie's water.

He whirled back and flung water in a wide arc. "Aaaargh! Stay back!"

Then to Silvie. "Douse your hair and your back!"

"What if we run out of water?"

"We'll take that risk. Douse them!"

The sound of splashing water followed immediately; she hadn't needed much encouragement. Johnis cupped cool liquid in his palm and dumped it on his head, then on his shoulders. As long as they remained wet, the bats would not touch them.

They each had three bags and were on their first. The way Johnis had explained it, one bag each for the journey in, one for the lair, the last for the escape. But they didn't know how deep the hole went or if this path really did lead to the lair. And with the dousing, the water in his bag was more than half-gone.

"You good?" he yelled.

"I'm in hell," she panted. "Alive, but not good."

"Good. Keep the extra bags wet too."

They pounded in, deeper, deeper, until the light that had peeked through twisted branches was darkened by the massive overhang they'd seen from above. The Black Forest had gone underground. They plunged ahead into pitch blackness.

"Just keep yourself wet!" Johnis yelled.

He could hear them, flapping and wheezing on every side. He could feel the wind from their wings when they swooped in close, missing him by mere inches. He could smell the putrid, sulfuric stench that stuffed his nostrils, forcing him to breathe through his mouth to keep from retching.

But he could see nothing. Fighting a fresh wave of panic, Johnis dumped more water on his head, rubbed more on his arms, splashed his face, his shoulders, his thighs.

"Johnis?"

The frantic tone in Silvie's voice betrayed her own fear.

"Are you wet?" he demanded. "Your thighs and sides, everything. Keep wet."

"I'm running out of water!"

The tip of a talon brushed Johnis's cheek, and he jerked back. The offending creature screeched, then hit a tree with a dull thump.

What if they tried suicide runs? Blasting in with claws outstretched knowing they would die on contact but killing him in the process?

No, they are too selfish to consider anything so noble, he decided.

"Good?" he called.

Silvie didn't respond. He could hear her breathing loudly, but she wasn't answering.

"Silvie! Are you good?"

"Don't ask such stupid questions."

They pounded deeper, deeper.

Johnis didn't know what they would find. He only knew that Darsal had come here looking for a book. The fact that they hadn't found any tracks headed back toward the forests meant she was still here somewhere, either dead or alive. Unless she had found a book and followed Billos, in which case she was somewhere else, either alive or dead.

Beyond that he could only make wild guesses, of which he'd made a hundred since the Roush Hunter had bounced up and down with the news of Darsal's betrayal.

His mount pulled up sharply and came to a stop. The air had gone strangely quiet. The musky smell of muddy water announced a change.

"We're out of the forest," Silvie said, breathing hard. "This is the lake?"

Johnis glanced up and saw them then, a hundred thousand sets of red eyes above and extending around what must be their lake.

He looked ahead and now just barely saw the dim reflection of so many eyes in the dark water. "This is it." But he couldn't see which way the path went.

He tried to force his horse left. It snorted and backed up. Right. This time it walked reluctantly forward.

"This way. How much water do you have left?"

"I'm on my second bag," Silvie said.

"Already?"

"You said keep yourself wet."

"I didn't say take a shower."

"I'm alive."

The horses kept to the darkened path, which gradually made its way around the lake. Johnis's eyes began to make out more details: the ring of leafless trees that bordered the lake; the black water, perfectly still without a breeze or a creature to move the surface; the thousands of red eyes, peering down, mostly in silence now.

And then the faint outline of a platform ahead as the path widened so that the horses could walk side by side.

"You see that?" he whispered.

"I see it," Silvie said next to him. "It looks familiar."

They'd seen another one of these platforms above Teeleh's lair. Though the Shataiki seemed to be imitating Elyon's creation of the forests and lakes, they were limited in their expression. Where Elyon's forests were circular and green, the Shataiki's were circular but black. Elyon's lakes were blue with a hint of green; Teeleh's dark and nasty. The Roush lived above the ground in the open air.

Teeleh's lair was deep underground.

"Let's pray we're right about the lair," Johnis said.

"Did you ever think you'd pray to find hell?"

He hesitated. It was madness. But then this whole business with the books had been madness from the start.

The horses stopped at the edge of the round platform. The air had grown even quieter.

"Now what?" Silvie whispered.

"Bring your water." Johnis swung off his horse, hoisted both bags of water from the saddlebag, and faced the platform, joined by Silvie.

"The horses?" she asked.

Good question. "We don't have enough water for them. Can't cover every angle, can we?"

He started to his right, following the platform's edge.

"That's a pretty important angle, wouldn't you say?" Silvie demanded, hurrying up beside him.

"Shataiki have no taste for horse meat," he said.

The form of the lair's opening loomed to his left. It reminded Johnis of the opening to the root cellars Thomas Hunter had suggested they build to store up food. Like a mouth in the ground.

He reached a trembling hand forward, felt for a handle, then pulled the door open. It creaked, not loudly, but easily heard above the still lake.

They stared into a darkness even thicker. Oily. A complete absence of light.

Silvie's cool fingers touched his elbow. Gripped him tight. "Are you sure about this?"

"Douse yourself," he said.

They both scooped fresh water over their heads.

"This feels wrong, Johnis," Silvie said.

"You want to go back then?"

Silence.

"Follow me," Johnis said and mounted the steps that led down into the lair.

twenty-seven

The first thing Billos saw upon exiting All Right Convenience was the empty warrior buggy sitting in front of Smither's Barbeque. Cops, Black had called them. A cop buggy.

No sign of anyone else on the streets. A face stared out from a window in the house across the street. Another person stood at the corner of a large temple-looking structure, watching him. The commoners had cleared the streets, knowing that Billos had suhupow at his fingertips. Still, it was amazing to him that there weren't more warriors crowding the streets.

It struck him in that moment that there was something amiss with this place called Paradise. It reminded him more of a staging from one of Thomas Hunter's battle schools than a fully formed village. No matter, he had his objective.

TED DEKKER

He strode for the eatery, gun held up by his right ear, ready for the slightest presentation of the enemy. He leapt up the steps and spun once to make sure he had the time he needed to do what needed doing.

Still no warriors on the street. Good.

He whirled for the door, threw it wide, and went in, gun blasting before the door had fully opened. *Boom, boom!* A beat. *Boom!*

Billos took care of where he sent his suhupow, of course. Two cops held guns on Darsal, who'd handed her weapon over to them. Their distraction by whatever threat they assumed she represented gave him the moment he needed to cut through them both.

They staggered back, clutching their chests. They slammed into the bar behind them and fell to the ground like dumped firewood.

Dead by Billos.

He swiveled the gun on the large Scab. Hesitated for only a moment. Then pulled the trigger.

The boom crashed around his ears, and Papa toppled backward. He landed with a thud that shook the whole building.

Dead by Billos.

"What?" Karas dove at the Scab's laid-out body. "Papa!"

"Papa's dead," Billos snapped. "As you will be if you don't do exactly what I say."

The power of his own dominance was nearly suffocating. Until that moment Billos wasn't sure what he would do, but feeling the gun buck in his hand and seeing the bodies drop, he now knew.

198

"You killed him!" Karas screamed. "Why'd you kill him?"

"Because he annoyed me. As do you. Now, kindly hand me the books and . . ."

The shelf where he'd seen the books was now bare.

Billos whirled and looked at Darsal for the first time since entering. "Where are the books?"

"You didn't take them?"

"Where are they?" he screamed.

"You tell me, O Wise Slayer of Men," she retorted, eyes fiery.

He knew her well enough to be sure she was immovable. Either she didn't know where the books were, or she had decided that the knowledge would remain with her.

"Then you'll be kind enough to walk ahead of me, out the back, before the warriors crash in and kill us all."

"I can see you've taken complete leave of your senses," she said.

"Why did you kill Papa?" Karas asked again.

Billos directed a blast of suhupow toward the shelves behind the bar. *Boom!* Glass shattered; bottles crashed to the ground.

"Move it! I'm not beyond taking a limb in this state of mind."

"Why not just kill us and be done with it?" Darsal demanded.

Billos hesitated, then spoke what he thought must be the truth. "Because I still love you."

"Love me? With a suhupow gun pointed at me?"

"You'll see. This will all make perfect sense when it's over. I'm chosen, Darsal. I was born for power, and this is the time of my making."

She refused to budge.

Billos shifted his gun so that it lined up with Karas. "Don't make me."

Darsal spit to one side, turned her back on him, and walked for the back door.

"You too." He motioned at Karas with the weapon.

"I don't know what kind of love you think this is, and I certainly don't know why Darsal ever loved anyone as mean as you," she snapped. Then she fell in behind Darsal.

Billos paraded them out of Smither's Barbeque, down the now-empty back alley, and through the store's back entrance.

"You see, now we're back to where we started," he said. "If you would have listened to me, Papa and the two cops would still be alive."

"We are listening to you," Darsal said. "And there's no doubt but that plenty of death awaits us all."

Billos searched the store for Marsuvees Black. That the man was putting him through this incredible test of loyalty, forcing Billos to betray Darsal, could only mean that what lay ahead was equally incredible.

Surely Black could have walked into the eatery and done what he wanted rather than give Billos the task. This was like battle school, and Billos was being put through the final test before being handed the sword of power.

As soon as Billos had proven himself, Black would undoubtedly give Darsal her freedom, and all would be forgiven. There was always the chance that Billos was wrong on this point, but he refused to take that slim chance seriously.

"Stop," he ordered.

Still no sign of Black.

"He wanted you to get the books for him, didn't he?" Darsal asked, turning to face him.

Billos wasn't sure what he was expected to do at this point. Maybe leave them locked up while he went after the rest of the village.

"He's after the books, Billos. For all we know, he's the Dark One. You're making a terrible mistake."

Billos had considered the possibility but refused to dwell on it. The lure of greatness was too great to be bothered by such unlikely risks. And even if it wasn't that unlikely . . . Billos had been chosen, what could he say?

"He's going to eat you up and spit you out," Darsal said.

"You're as smart as you look, peach plum."

Billos turned to face Marsuvees Black, who stood with legs spread, arms crossed, watching hard. There had been no sound of entry, but then Billos hardly expected any. The man moved in mysterious ways.

"I brought them," Billos said.

"Did you, now? Did I want the flesh alone? No. The word became flesh. I need the word. Where are the books?"

"So this is Black?" Darsal said. "Looks like the Dark One to me. A human form of Teeleh himself."

"Teeleh?" Black cocked his head and flashed Darsal a wicked grin. "Do tell."

Darsal didn't look like she was interested in backing down.

"Don't make trouble," Billos snapped at her. To Black: "The books—"

"Shut your slit. I said, 'Do tell.' Does that sound like an order to zip her yapper? Now, do . . . tell."

Billos wasn't sure what to make of Black's perturbed nature.

"Teeleh," Darsal said, "the black winged beast who leads the Shataiki, where we come from. An evil bat who despises Elyon, the creator of the Great Romance and all that is good."

"You're suggesting that I'm *not* good?" Black asked, stunned. "Me . . ."—he spread his fingers and pressed them on his chest— "not a bowl of cherries on a cool summer's eve? Not a butterfly who whistles 'Dixie' in the face of the coming storm? Not a worm dancing in a top hat with a grin as wide as the moon?" He took a calming breath. "How dare you suggest I'm not all those things. And more."

The images made no sense to Billos. More suhupow talk. The power that rolled off Black's tongue was enough to make a grown warrior surrender his sword.

"And for the record," Black continued, "where you come from is *here*. If you die here, you die. If, on the other hand, you help me retrieve the books, I'll let you live."

"Find the books yourself," Darsal said.

"Unfortunately, due to a small glitch in the system, they aren't available to me. For that I have chosen Billos. Isn't that right, chosen one?"

Billos blinked. "Yes. That's right."

"I'm begging you, Billos." Darsal's eyes pleaded. "You're making a terrible mistake!"

"Stop it!" Billos snapped. She was going to ruin everything! Even if she was right, they were now thoroughly committed to whatever path of glory Black had chosen him for. "You're not thinking clearly."

"It's you who's lost his mind!" Karas cried.

They all looked at the young girl, who stood small to one side.

"They're waiting, Billy-baby," Black said. He nodded at the door. "Lead them outside to the back of the church. The lynching party's waiting there."

"For what?"

"For a lynching. Not you. Them."

"I thought you wanted me to kill the villagers . . ."

The muscles on Black's jaw bunched. "I've changed my mind. A grown man's got that prerogative, don't you think? Give me the books now, and I might change my mind again."

So this was Black's game. He was forcing Billos's hand.

"I don't have the books!"

A dark shadow crossed Black's face. His lips flattened. "Paradise has a history of lynching, and today's starting to feel like a history lesson."

It's a test. And I'm no fool. Billos faced Darsal, torn between frustration and anger. "Satisfied? Where are the books?"

"Even if I did know—"

"Outside," Black said. He snapped his fingers. "Take a look."

Billos looked from Darsal to Black, then back.

"Now you're starting to irritate me," Black said.

Billos crossed the room, put his hand on the doorknob, and pulled the door open, expecting to see a posse of cops waiting with drawn guns.

Instead he faced a windblown street, covered by sand. Black storm clouds crowded the sky so low that the instinct to crouch made him flinch. The buildings were stripped of their colors, and the glass was broken on most of them. The town had changed with the snap of Black's fingers.

But what surprised Billos the most were the villagers. Two dozen, gathered on the street facing the store. Clothes tattered. Staring hard, with slits for eyes.

Their flesh looked to be bloodied and rotting. Like human Horde, without the disease. They were half-dead, maybe all dead. Others were joining solemnly, filling the street behind.

The lynching party.

"Welcome to my world," the magic man said behind him.

Billos twisted back.

But Black was gone.

twenty-eight

Darsal could see the mob over Billos's shoulder, and she knew that her worst fears were about to come to pass. She glanced back with Billos and was surprised to see that the man dressed in the black trench coat was gone. He'd simply vanished.

She spun back to Billos, who was staring outside again. He stood with his back toward her and Karas, weapon pointed at the floor.

He was a handsome seventeen-year-old with dark hair and bright eyes, muscled from neck to heel, able to swing a sword through the chests of five Horde in one terrible swoop. A man of seventeen, ready to take a wife. To take Darsal as his wife.

Yet here in this crazy land of the white room where DELL played with their minds, he was a child swept away with the promise of power at whatever cost—it hardly mattered.

"Billos."

He didn't turn.

"Billos!" Karas snapped. "You big thug, listen to her!"

He whirled, angry. "It's a test, you fools!"

"And if you're wrong?" Karas demanded.

But Billos wasn't listening. "Hey!" he called out to the mob.

"Send her out," a large blond-headed one at the mob's center said. The skin on his face was peeling, revealing black flesh beneath.

A thin, wiry warrior, who looked like he might be quicker than a snake, stepped up beside the large blond. "Let me take 'em all. I can take 'em; you know I can."

"Shut up, Pete."

Another man stepped up, hands spread by his hips, as if he expected suhupow to fill them at the slightest movement. The look in his narrowed eyes put a chill in Darsal's neck. She knew their kind—warriors who lived for the love of blood more than any cause. In the Forest Guard they were called throaters: fighters who counted their value by the number of Scab throats they'd cut.

Scanning the gathering mob, Darsal saw that at least half of them looked to be throaters. They were here for vengeance, and they would not go home without their fill of blood.

"Who are you?" Billos demanded.

The leader hesitated. "Claude."

"What will you do with them?"

"We're going to string them up," the man called Claude said

matter-of-factly. "By their necks. We want to watch them twitch in the air."

The wind gusted past the door.

"What if I give you one of them?" Billos asked. "The young one?"

Darsal wasn't sure she'd heard him correctly. This was Billos, for the sake of Elyon!

"Three is better," Claude said, stepping forward. "Father, son, and all."

Darsal had no clue what he was talking about.

"The last time we just went with the one, the son, and it cost us," Claude said.

"I hear you," Billos said. "So you want to string them both up?"

"Are you deaf?" asked Claude.

Darsal had crossed the desert, traded her soul to Alucard, betrayed Thomas, all for Billos's sake. But she knew that if she didn't make a move now, they would all die. And since Billos wasn't moving with her, she would have to work alone.

She caught Karas's eye and looked to the rear exit. The young girl nodded. Darsal eased back toward the door, moving to her right as she did so, until the door frame blocked the view of the mob.

"I hear you." Billos shoved his gun into its holster. He snapped his fingers, and a glass goblet magically appeared in his hand. "I hear you, and I'll drink to that."

Amazing. Darsal briefly wondered what it felt like to have that kind of power. She bumped into the door behind her, and the questions fled. Reaching for the knob, she cracked the door soundlessly, then slipped outside, followed by Karas.

She had the presence of mind to shut the door in the face of the blowing wind before running across the back alley and into the forest behind. She rounded a crowded bunch of trees and pulled up hard.

"He's gone mad!" Karas whispered, sliding in beside her.

"Watch your tongue."

"Just because you love him doesn't mean he isn't mad. Now what?"

"We have to get the books." Darsal paced, frantic.

"Get the books and leave him?"

"If you think I would ever leave Billos, you're as mad as he is."

"So you admit he's mad? But the fact that you risked your neck to get this far is clouding your judgment."

"Was Johnis's judgment clouded when he went back for you?"

That put her back on her heels. She stared into the forest for a moment, then looked up at Darsal. "I wanted to be saved. You can't help someone who doesn't want help."

"You're assuming his desires won't change," Darsal snapped.

"What do you see in him? He's not the lovable kind."

"Zip it! What does a child know about love? There's no way this side of Teeleh's breath that I'm leaving Billos. Don't say another word of it!"

"Nice," Karas quipped. "And dangerous too."

"What is?"

"Love," Karas said.

A loud boom ripped through the air. They both started and faced the village.

"Billos?"

BILLOS RELEASED THE GOBLET, LETTING IT CRASH ON THE floorboards. He stared at the broken glass shards at his feet. The feeling of raw power that accompanied every snap of his fingers was positively intoxicating. A small part of his mind knew that he was stalling, but the greater part of his heart was so wrapped up in ambition that he couldn't bring his thoughts to focus on that corner of his thinking.

"Okay," he said, looking up. "If you—"

The words caught in his throat. Claude had lifted his long-barreled weapon and was staring at him as if *he* were the enemy.

"Cut them off behind," Claude ordered.

Four villagers broke from the mob and jogged two to each side of the building, watching Billos as they disappeared into the alley behind.

At any other time, in any battle with any of the Horde, Billos wouldn't have mistaken the move as anything but a clear threat. At the moment, however, he wasn't thinking clearly, and worse, he knew it. He couldn't make his mind work fast enough.

They were throaters. Any fool could see that much. But what

direct threat these particular throaters posed to him wasn't clear, at least not to him.

Black's order drummed through his mind. *Kill them all, every last one of them. Baby.* His guns were still in his hip holsters. But he wasn't in the business of killing them all right at this moment. He was in the business of giving them what they wanted.

He glanced over his shoulder. Saw the room was empty.

Gone? Darsal had betrayed him?

The rear door crashed open and filled with two of the four snakes who'd covered the alley. A quick glance told the story.

"They're gone!" the one on the right called. He was dressed in a blue shirt stained with something black, maybe blood from the long cut on his cheek, maybe Horde sap for all Billos knew.

. But his mind was working well enough now to know that things were turning bad.

The two snakes spread out and made room for the other two. All four drilled him with piercing glares, hands spread above the butts of their weapons.

"You'll do," Claude growled.

Billos faced him, every instinct now on razor's edge. This was it, then. He'd failed in this one simple test because Darsal had betrayed him, and now instead of being the aggressor in an offensive posture, he was hopelessly surrounded by an enemy too overwhelming to even consider engaging directly.

But you are the chosen one, Billos. And you were chosen for a reason.

He spread his hands in a gesture of reconciliation and slowly stepped onto the boardwalk. "Okay, settle down. You want to lynch me? Fine. You can string me up and watch me twitch in the air."

Billos walked directly toward them, ignoring the trembling in his legs. He didn't know how much power waited between his fingers, or how much power Claude and the company of snakes who were poised to string him up had between theirs.

But he was about to find out.

"Why not make a sport of it, though?" he said.

The dark sky hung low overhead. Sand blew across the ground.

"Pete seems pretty eager to take me on. Let him. One-on-one. Better yet, I'll take two of you on."

Claude stared at him, no doubt taken off guard by such a bold suggestion. But he wasn't agreeing.

"Five, then," Billos said, halting ten feet from the man. "Put me in a circle with five men."

"Let's do him," one of the throaters said, stepping up. He held a sharpened stake, roughly three feet in length, in each hand. "Let's stick him."

"Back off, Roland. He's a trickster."

"But only one trickster," Billos said.

"We can take him, Dad," Pete said.

Billos glanced behind the men and calmly took in the specifics of his predicament. His fingers tingled with anticipation. Oddly enough, he felt his fear slip away, replaced only with a thirst to see just how much power Black had lit in his hands.

The chosen one. It had a haunting sound.

"Pete's right. This whole lynching party is a sham. I could take you all with a single sword!" Billos declared.

"Swords don't do the trick here. The only way you win is to turn the girl over to us; that's the way it goes."

The. Chosen. One.

"I don't think so, Claude." Billos held both hands out like a priest welcoming his flock. "I'll tell you what I think. I think . . ." He snapped his fingers. Cold steel filled both palms. Twin guns in addition to the one on his hip.

A bolt of adrenaline ripped down his spine, and in that single brief moment, Billos knew that he had found his calling. He regretted having ditched the black coat and hat, because in truth he was nothing less than the magic man, Marsuvees Black himself.

The. Chosen. One.

The thoughts crashed through his mind in the space of half a heartbeat, and then he was moving, faster than lightning. He dove to his right and sent two bullets, one from each gun, while he was in the air.

They struck each mark in the forehead, two of the snakes with long guns next to Claude. The long guns first, then the handguns.

Both warriors dropped like lifeless dolls, dead by Billos.

He landed on his shoulder and was twisting back for the four throaters behind him when the first bullets smacked into the dirt near his head, spraying his cheek.

Moving like a viper, he whipped around with both guns and sent the suhupow—the bullets—*boom, boom, boom, boom!*

The four throaters had their guns out, firing, running full tilt toward him, zigzagging to spoil his aim, but Billos made the appropriate adjustments on the fly. The power from his hands smashed into their foreheads and knocked them clean off their feet.

Watching it, Billos knew he was a god. Slayer of throaters. Chosen by Black to kick . . .

Something tugged at his arm. He'd been hit?

But this didn't slow Billos down. He was rolling like a log, feeling the ground around his body thump with bullets from the mob. Rolling toward the corner of the building to his right. Having eliminated the throaters, Billos had no concern of a rear attack. All he had to do was reach cover and he would win this first round.

A second tug smarted him, this one on his left leg. Then he spun past the corner, chased by the staccato beats of bullets smacking into the wood.

Billos leapt to his feet and glanced at his leg to see a flesh wound that added no concern. They'd struck him twice, but both hits were superficial. And he'd slain six of the snakes.

Thirty to go. Roughly.

"Round the back!" Claude's voice snarled. "Split up, and make sure he doesn't—"

Billos moved then before they could possibly expect a second attack. He jumped back into the open, firing as he cleared the corner, pulling the levers as fast as he could move his fingers. Faster than he could have imagined. The guns thundered in rapid succession, rolling bolts of lightning. Like drumsticks beating the low-hung clouds.

Billos was aware of each volley, each hit, each thrasher thrown from his feet. Each return shot spinning past him as he rushed directly at the mob.

There were seven long guns, and he took them out first, ending with one held by a graying woman who wore a fierce scowl. The bullet dropped her to the ground, scowl still in place.

God has spoken. Baby.

No sign of Claude, Billos realized as he cleared the corner of Smither's Barbeque. The large blond-headed leader had perhaps made his way to the back without Billos noticing.

He pulled up with his back against the side boards and glanced both directions. The street had gone quiet in the wake of his bold attack. No less than twelve of them now lay on the ground, dead by Billos.

"Kill them all," Black had said. And Billos intended to show him how easily he could do it. As easy as slicing through the Horde.

An image of Darsal skipped through his mind, then was gone. In good time she would understand. He could be wrong, misguided by his own passion to seize power, deceived, as she claimed. But he didn't want to think about that. Not now. Not when he had the rest of the village to level.

A raspy chuckle cackled through the air, stilling Billos in his boots. It came from the street around the corner, and it sounded very much like Black.

With the throaters?

Then his name, long and low. "Billieeeeeeeee . . ."

Not his name exactly, but the same name Black had called him once or twice.

"Billieeeeeeeeee . . . Olly Olly Oxen Free. Come to Papa, baby."

"You heard him."

Billos spun around and found himself staring into twin barrels only inches from his face. Holding the long gun was Claude, eyes fiery with anticipation.

Billos acted out of an instinct bred from thousands of fights in the Southern Forest as a lad, most of which he'd handily won. There was good reason he'd been selected by Thomas Hunter to lead the new recruits, and he would show it now.

He threw himself backward into a backflip, ducking beneath the weapon's line of fire and bringing his feet up in the same smooth motion.

Boom! The gun blast buffeted the air over his arched chest. His feet connected with Claude's arms, and he finished the full rotation before Claude's gun clattered to the ground. Now he faced a weaponless thug with round eyes.

"Dead by Billos," he said, and pulled both levers.

Click, click.

He blinked. The suhupow seemed to have fizzled. He jerked the levers again. *Click, click.*

"Billieeeeee . . ." Black's voice chuckled. "Come to Daddy, Billy-baby."

twenty-nine

Billos had two options: he could snap his fingers and make more suhupow, or he could trust Black and go to daddy, as the man suggested.

He dropped the guns on the ground, spun around, and walked out into the open. Black stood in the center of the street, arms and feet spread wide, grinning wickedly, trench coat whipped to one side by the gusting wind. His head was tilted down so that Billos could just see the whites of his eyes beneath the rim of his hat.

The throaters stood evenly on either side, staring at Billos, weapons lowered. Behind them the temple towered tall, nearly touching the black sky above.

"Hello, Billosssss," Black said. "Wanna trip? Wanna, wanna, baby?"

It is a test, Billos quickly decided. A final test to see how he would use his suhupow in the face of terrible odds.

"Do you want me to kill them all?" he called.

"Yes, Billos. Kill them all. Do it now."

So Billos snapped his fingers to fill them with steel and continue his reign of terror, to make them all dead by Billos. But this time a small glitch sidelined the plan.

This time no steel filled his hands.

He snapped again, harder.

The snaps clicked over the whistling wind.

"What's the matter, baby?" Black said. "A little low on grace-juice, are we?"

What was he saying? The suhupow was gone? Billos felt the blood drain from his face. His mind fogged. Surely . . . But he wasn't sure what he should be sure about.

Something nudged his back. Claude had retrieved his long gun and was prodding him.

"What's happening?" he asked.

"You don't know?"

"No."

"No? No, Billossssssss. You really don't know, do you? You worthless slug."

"What . . ."

"The girl is what," Black said. "I asked you to give me the girl. It was all so simple. You waltzed into town like you owned the place and laid four of them in the grave. Now they need a lynching to satisfy their lust. A life for a life, that's the way it works here. I suggested the girl. Instead you're giving them someone else. Your call, not mine."

"Who?"

Black cocked his head. "Please don't tell me this disease named idiocy has gone that far. Or are you seeing double, baby? Because I only see one of you."

Billos felt dizzy. He snapped his fingers, knowing nothing would happen. There was still a chance; there had to be. This was still a test of some kind.

But for the first time the suggestions Darsal had made spoke louder than his own confidence. There was a possibility that Black's motives were less than noble.

He looked around quickly, searching for options. Could he dodge Claude's gun again and make a run for it? But five others had now joined the large man. And those on either side of Black were spreading out to encircle him.

He faced the magic man and stepped forward. "Hold on. I thought . . . I thought we had a deal."

"Didn't your mommy tell you never to make a deal with the devil? What I give I can take. String him up!"

Behind him, Claude grunted, and something crashed into the back of Billos's head. He felt himself falling, but was out before he hit the ground.

He came to slowly, to the sound of heavy breathing and the pain of twisted joints. Light filtered past his eyes, and he saw the sky above, black and boiling, just above the nearly bare branches of a large oak that hung over him like a menacing skeleton.

Something wet dripped on his face. Sweat from the flushed face of a throater who leaned over him, pulling on a rope they'd slung over the thickest branch high above.

The full realization of what he was up against hit Billos, and he jerked his legs in a moment of panic. Pain shot down his bones. They'd tied his arms and legs back like a hog's, so that any movement from his arms only pulled his legs back behind his hips and vice versa.

"String him up," Claude said.

"Wait!" Billos cried, or tried to cry—he managed only a grunt.

They hauled him up by a rope. He left the ground facedown, arms and legs arched behind his back, barely able to hold back his screams.

The rope jerked with each pull, sending stabs of pain through his joints.

He heard the cackling then, from a porch on the back side of the temple where they'd dragged him. Black watched with arms crossed, smiling.

"Go ahead and let it all out, baby. They deserve a scream."

Billos stared into the man's eyes, set above curling lips. Black eyes that didn't appear to have any pupils. And in those dark, oily pools, Billos could see himself screaming. Clawing his way up, as if the man's eye was a tunnel into the abyss, and he, Billos, was being sucked in.

He blinked, and the image was gone. Only Black now, smiling at him with shiny white teeth and dark eyes.

"The books, Billos," Black said. "I need the books."

"I . . . I don't know . . ."

The throaters tied the rope off to one of the porch posts, leaving Billos to sway a few feet above a large circle the men formed. The rope creaked above him.

Black paced, arms still crossed. "If that's the truth, then I have no use for you; you do realize that, don't you?"

He hadn't thought of it that way. Words failed him in the face of the pain. Below, one of the villagers approached, dragging the Scab's large Horde sword. He gripped it with both hands and looked up at Billos.

"Do you know what happens to the stomach when it's sliced open in your particular position?" Black asked.

It was with those words that Billos knew his fate was sealed. How he'd missed the plain signs along the way he didn't know, but his meeting Marsuvees Black had not been a chance encounter.

Billos had been warned that entering the books was dangerous, and he was now snared by that danger. Black was the Dark One, and he'd wanted nothing but the books the whole time. Now that Billos was powerless to deliver the books, Black would simply kill him.

"I believe you," Black said. "You're a complete idiot and know nothing. Which means you have only one slim chance. Short of that, you take the long trip to the place of wailing and gnashing of teeth."

Billos's vision blurred. *What have I done?* His heart broke, nine feet from the ground, facing down at death. And all he could think was, *What have I done?*

"Darsal," he croaked.

"The name's Black," the man said. "Marsuvees Black. Cut him up!"

The throater with the sword drew it back. One cut was all it would take to spill his intestines to the ground.

Billos began to weep.

"No! Let him go."

He twisted in his ropes and looked at Darsal, who stood beyond the circle of throaters, staring up at him.

Karas, the little girl, stepped up beside Darsal. "Let him go," she said, matching Darsal's intensity.

Darsal whispered something in harsh tones, but the young girl didn't appear interested in listening. She held her ground, jaw set.

Darsal faced Black. "I'm the one you want. I know where the books are. Take me."

"We're the ones you want. We know where the books are. Take us," the young girl repeated.

"Well, well, well," Black muttered. "Lucky for you, Billy-boy, fools come in pairs." Then louder so that they could all hear: "Cut him down!"

It took only a few jerky, painful moments for Billos to reach the ground again. But it was more than enough time for the implications of what was occurring to rack his mind.

Darsal was giving herself for him. Did she think she could survive the experience? Surely she wasn't doing this out of some misguided sense called "love." He couldn't accept that. Wouldn't accept that.

Two throaters hauled Billos to his feet, where he stood shakily.

"You may leave," Black said. "If I ever see you alive again, I'll fix the problem."

Claude shoved Darsal and Karas into the circle.

"Go, Billos," Darsal said.

"Darsal?" What could he say? "You can't do this."

"Go, Billos!" she snapped. "Before you do even more damage, just go!"

"And do what? I don't know where the books are! I can't get back! And what about you? I can't let them—"

"It's too late!" she interrupted. "Do you have any suhupow in your fingers?"

He snapped his fingers. The smack of his fingers against his palm sounded stupidly weak.

"Just go," she said. Tears filled her eyes. "Please, go now, before I change my mind."

Raw horror set into Billos's chest. He couldn't go, he realized. How could he live with the knowledge that Darsal had died for him?

223

"I can't," he said. A knot rose into his throat. "I can't, Darsal!"

He looked down at Karas, glaring at him through silent tears. She'd been saved only a few days ago and was now returning the favor for another. But not without a struggle. A misguided fool! And now a misguided fool on his conscience.

"I suppose I could have all three of you hanged," Black said. "Romeo and Juliet and all that crap."

"Go, you fool," Karas said. "I will do what I can to save my sister. Go before her sacrifice becomes meaningless!"

Billos took a step backward, fighting waves of remorse and fear all wrapped into one terrible bundle.

Darsal added her insistence. "Go!"

He blinked, unable to hold back streams of tears. "Darsal . . ."

"Go!" she screamed.

"I think she means it," Black said.

Billos stumbled forward, through the throaters who parted for him, to the corner of the temple, powerless to stop Black or Darsal or any of them, including himself.

"Kill the little girl first," Black said behind him.

They are both dead, he realized. *Dead by Billos.*

And then he ran blindly into the street, wishing it was he who was dead.

thirty

The stairs curved to Johnis's left as they descended, much the same as in Teeleh's lair. He guided himself by letting the tips of his right-hand fingers drag along the stones on his right, refusing to consider the makeup of the slippery, musky substance covering them.

Silvie rested her hand on his shoulder and followed close. Her breath was warm on his neck, and he drew a small amount of comfort from the human contact.

He stopped after a good twenty steps and stared ahead, trying to make something, anything, out. The odor down here was worse than above. He lifted his elbow to his nose and tried to get a few filtered draws of air without blanching, but his sleeve proved useless, so he gave up.

A sizzle on the steps below startled him. "What?"

"Water," Silvie said after a moment. "The ground doesn't like our water."

She was using more of the precious fluid and had spilled some on the stones, where it sizzled in protest.

"Don't use too much," Johnis said, resuming his descent.

The steps ended on flat ground in pitch darkness. Johnis felt his way toward a door on the right, again positioned in exactly the same place as in Teeleh's lair. They were each replicas of the same design.

He pulled the heavy door open and saw light for the first time. An orange glow ebbed and swayed in a tunnel to their right.

"It's the same as before," he said.

"You recognize it?" Her voice was thin and shaky.

Johnis took her hand. "Identical," he said. "This is his lair."

"Whose lair?"

"The prince or whatever they call him that rules this forest."

"Not Teeleh himself, then."

"I don't think so. Maybe. I think we'll know soon enough."

He led her forward, but she pulled her hand free after a few steps, preferring to keep the water bag close instead.

Johnis stopped when they saw the first worm on the tunnel wall. Ten feet long, perhaps three inches thick, sliding though its own milky mucus. He studied it for a moment, then flicked water on it.

The worm uttered a soft, alien shriek and thrashed on the

wall, skin smoking where the water had made contact. It fell to the ground with a loud splat that echoed down the tunnel.

Johnis looked at Silvie. Neither said a word. They went in, deeper.

The orange light was coming from a flame fixed to the entrance of what Johnis assumed was a library or a study, like the one in Teeleh's lair.

He stopped and nodded. "This is it."

"If Darsal's alive, she's staying quiet."

Johnis didn't want to dwell on the implications of the statement. It was bad enough that they'd seen no sign of their comrades since entering the Black Forest.

"Keep your water ready," he said, but he didn't need to. Silvie had her right hand submerged already.

They strode up to the gated entrance and found it open.

"Come in."

The voice was thin and rasped like a file on a sword. Johnis took out a dripping hand and stepped into the underground library.

The room was small, maybe ten paces square, with a bank of bookcases on his right, a short table in the center, and several stuffed chairs situated haphazardly around. A torch flame licked at the wall opposite the entrance. All very much like in Teeleh's lair.

But the tall, mangy Shataiki seated at the desk to Johnis's left was not Teeleh.

"I knew you would eventually make it," the Shataiki said.

"Alucard," Silvie whispered.

"You remember."

The bat stood. He was taller than most Shataiki by a foot or two, but shorter than Teeleh by as much. Thinner, much thinner. His mangy carcass hung off his bones like cobwebs. Vivid images of what this creature had done to them sent shivers down Johnis's spine.

"I could kill you," Johnis said.

Alucard lowered his eyes to the water bag in Johnis's hands. "Yes, I suppose you could. You're growing more clever by the day."

The bat had no fear, which could only mean he knew something they did not.

"Where's Darsal?"

"You amaze me, you humans," Alucard said. "All this way to save one lousy slab of meat? You're not fearless; I can see that by the twitching of your lips, however slight. Which means you're facing your fears. A noble thing."

"Loyalty," Johnis said. "Something you have no inkling about."

"True. I would as quickly slit Teeleh's throat as yours; he knows that. But I can't."

"Darsal," Johnis snapped. "If you can't lead me to her, you're worthless to me."

"So you come into my home with your precious water and play master."

"I have no interest in being your master."

Alucard sat down and turned back to a book on his desk. The torch cast light over an obscured title. "Your friends aren't here," the Shataiki said. "They left with a very precious possession of mine."

"One of the books," Johnis said.

"Do you know what the books can do?" Alucard asked, tracing a single black talon over the cover of the book in front of him. Then he told them, relishing his words.

"All seven and the rules which bind them are broken. Used together the original seven books can undo it all."

"For evil," Silvie said. "I wouldn't think you'd need the books to ply your trade."

"Not just evil." Alucard turned his head and stared at them with red eyes, unable to hide the smirk on his jaw. "Good always wins. You wonder why? Because it's more powerful. Evil ultimately leads to the discovery of good. Even the death of the Maker would end in some kind of good." He spat a thick wad of green mucus at the wall, where it slowly slid down to the floor.

"But all seven books used together changes that. The glory is hardly imaginable. It would change everything." Alucard slammed a fist on the desk. "Everything!"

"The Dark One seeks seven," Johnis muttered.

"The Dark One." Alucard chuckled, a phlegm-popping, raspy affair. "Unfortunately, only four of the books are here. Or should I say were here before your friends disappeared with them. A bad thing, because those four are needed to find the three books in the lesser reality."

Johnis knew he was learning more than he could hope to understand in one sitting. Being here in this underground lair was maybe not as much a consequence of Billos's indiscretion as part of their mission to find the books.

"What lesser reality?" Silvie asked.

"Open a book and find out. And it's not the place your friends went off to, not unless they have all four and opened one, in which case we're all wasting time."

A faint clicking sound ran down the tunnel behind them. Johnis focused his thoughts on the task at hand. Darsal.

"She's not here. Then why shouldn't I just kill you and leave?"

"Because I'm not as stupid as your friends," Alucard said. "You think I would just hand over my sole book out of kindness?"

"What have you done?"

"It's not me. Darsal took the book after making a binding vow on the books to return all four to me if she is able to find Billos."

Johnis felt his pulse surge. "Or?"

"She is mine," Alucard said.

"Not good," Silvie said.

The statement needed no response and received none.

"So then I should kill you."

"Then by the bond of her vow, Darsal will share my fate. Kill me, and you kill her."

True? Johnis didn't know, but the notion had a ring of authenticity to it.

Alucard continued. "You're alive because you have the water, but it won't last forever. If I were you, I'd head out now, while you still have an advantage."

Hearing Alucard speak with such reasoned skill cast him in a totally different light than the Shataiki Johnis had suffered under in Teeleh's forest or the one who'd sat upon Witch's head in the Horde city. Alucard was an enemy to be feared. And at the moment, he had spoken the truth. They had to get out of the Black Forest while they still had water. Once in the desert, they could regroup with Hunter.

Johnis stepped back. "Let's go, Silvie." To Alucard: "Just know that in the end, Elyon honors his chosen ones."

The bat cackled, unimpressed.

Johnis backed out of the library, eyes on the beast who drilled him with a red stare.

"Johnis?"

He spun at Silvie's urgent tone. The source of the clicking he'd heard earlier suddenly became apparent: dozens of worms sliding slowly toward them from deeper underground. The clicking was their popping of mucus.

This was no place for them.

"Go!"

No further encouragement needed, they ran toward the entrance together. Out into the atrium. Into darkness again. Up the stone steps, sloshing water as they stumbled forward.

Out into the open air.

"This way!" Johnis said, veering back toward the horses. The bats still ringed the lake, even more now than before. A hundred thousand, maybe two hundred thousand. A sea of red eyes peering in silence except for the odd hissing.

"Save your water . . ."

It was as far as Johnis got. He slid to a halt and stared ahead into the dim glow of red. The horses lay on their sides, butchered and stripped of flesh.

"They're dead!" Silvie cried.

An understatement.

The hissing and clicking from the trees swelled as the Shataiki became aware that their deed had been discovered. Still, not one of them moved.

"We'll never make it out on foot," Silvie said. "We don't have enough water!"

"We have to go back down," Johnis said.

Silvie stared at him. Then at her horse.

They both knew that he was right.

thirty-one

Billos ran blind into the blowing wind, across the center of the town, past Smither's Barbeque, and into the alley before pulling up, panting. He spun back and tried to make sense of what was happening, but his mind wasn't working right.

His heart, on the other hand, was pumping on overload, shoving pain through his veins. Details that seemed so vague only minutes ago now sat vividly on the horizon of his mind, like statues to the dead.

He'd accepted the invitation of the Dark One to enter the books and had woken in a place in which Black gave and took powers to serve his purpose. But it was Billos's own ambition that had blinded him to the danger.

Darsal had seen what he had not. Like a child ignoring his

father's warning not to touch the fire, Billos had touched, had shoved his hand into the flames, had thrown his body onto the coals.

He paced, scrambling for a course of action that made sense, snapping his fingers uselessly. A gun still hung on his hip, but one futile pull of its lever and he knew the suhupow was gone forever. Without it he didn't stand a chance against the throaters, whose guns would still shoot this suhupow called bullets.

"Darsal . . ." Billos whimpered, hands gripped in fists. He paced, desperate to be dead, his only escape now. But Black didn't want him, not even as a sacrifice for Darsal. Only Elyon knew what atrocity was building behind that temple.

Billos lifted his chin to the black sky, let his mouth open in the face of the wind, and sank slowly to his knees. His body shook with each sob, but each cry only brought a greater sense of finality.

A lone cry drifted on the wind. It was light and too high-pitched to be Darsal. Why had the stubborn wench insisted on offering herself as well? Wasn't Darsal enough? Karas was a fool, a Scab pretending to be clean, a runt of a girl who had no business being here.

But all of that was a lie! Karas was his savior! He would worship the thought of her, give his life to save those like her. Elyon, Elyon, how foolish had he been? Billos wailed at the sky.

"Hello, Billos."

He started and jerked his head to his right. The young blond-headed boy who'd warned him about the Dark One stood in the alley, hands limp by his side. Samuel.

"Now do you believe me?" the boy asked.

Billos gripped his hair in both hands, lowered his head so that his chin rested on his chest, clenched his eyes tight, and cried to cover his shame.

"There is a way, you know," the boy said.

Billos looked up. "What? It's hopeless! They're dead already!"

"For you, I mean," Samuel said. "It might be too late for them, but there may be a way for you."

"I don't need a way!"

"That's your first mistake. You need a way more than they do."

"Black has them!" he snapped angrily. "How can you say that?"

"No. Black has you, Billos."

Whether it was the use of his name or the way that Samuel said it with such authority, Billos wasn't sure. But he knew that his whole life was somehow wrapped up in those simple words. *Black has you, Billos.*

The wind seemed to ease, quieted by the moment. Samuel stared at him with green eyes that drew him with their absolute surety.

"Do you want this?" the boy asked.

Billos pushed himself to his feet. Everything went quiet except for the thumping of his heart. The green of Samuel's eyes begged him to run, to leap into a water that would wash away the darkness Black had filled him with.

"I can give you something that makes his suhupow seem silly."

"Yes," Billos said.

Samuel's lips twisted into a tempting grin. "Are you sure?"

"Yes. Yes, show me."

"Follow me."

Samuel spun on his heels and bounded barefoot toward the forest. He glanced over his shoulder, grinning wide. "Come on!"

Billos stumbled forward, then ran after the boy. Into the forest. Following glimpses of Samuel, who raced ahead, leaping over fallen logs, crashing through the brush like a deer.

The wind was gone here, held back by the trees, replaced by the sound of Billos's feet cracking twigs and his lungs pulling at the air. There was something familiar about the trees here. A scent that seemed common to him. If he didn't know better he might have guessed that he was back in Middle Forest, racing after a Roush.

The boy was leaving him behind. "Wait!"

But there was no need for Samuel to wait, because the trees ended. Billos slid to a halt at the shore of a brilliant green lake surrounded by emerald trees.

The boy was halfway down the sandy beach, sprinting for a large rock set half in the sand, half in the water. Billos watched in amazement as Samuel launched himself up onto the rock and then catapulted himself into a beautifully arched dive.

For a moment he seemed to hang suspended, and then he plunged into the green waters with hardly a splash.

Billos stood panting from the run, waiting for the boy to reemerge, wondering if he was supposed to follow. But he knew the answer already. The lake, like the boy's eyes, begged him to run. To jump. To dive deep.

Billos ran. He tore down the shore, bounded up on the rock, and dove into the air.

The instant Billos hit the water, his body shook violently. A blue strobe exploded in his eyes, and he knew that he was going to die. That he had entered a forbidden pool, pulled by the wrong desire, and now he would pay with his life.

The warm water engulfed him. Flutters rippled through his body and erupted into a boiling heat that knocked the wind from his lungs. The shock alone might kill him.

But it was pleasure that surged through his body, not pain. Pleasure! The sensations coursed through his bones in great unrelenting waves.

Elyon.

How he was certain, he did not know. But he knew. Elyon was in this lake with him.

Billos opened his eyes. Gold light drifted by. He lost all sense of direction. The water pressed in on every inch of his body, as intense as any acid, but one that burned with pleasure instead of pain.

His violent shaking gave way to a gentle trembling as he sank into the water. He opened his mouth and laughed. He wanted more, much more. He wanted to suck the water in and drink it.

Without thinking he did that. He took a great gulp and then inhaled. The liquid hit his lungs. Billos pulled up, panicked. He tried to hack the water from his lungs, but inhaled more instead. No pain. He carefully sucked more water and breathed it out slowly. Then again, deep and hard. Out with a soft whoosh. He was breathing the water! In great heaves he was breathing the lake's intoxicating water.

Billos shrieked with laughter. He tumbled through the water, pulling his legs in close so he would roll, and then stretching them out so he thrust forward, farther into the colors surrounding him. He swam into the lake, deeper and deeper, twisting and rolling with each stroke. The power contained in this lake was far greater than anything he'd ever imagined.

I made this, Billos.

Billos pulled up. He whipped his body around, searching for the words' source. A giggle rippled though the water. Billos grinned stupidly and spun around.

"Elyon?" His voice was muffled, hardly a voice at all.

Do you like it?

The words reached into his bones, and he began to tremble again. He wasn't sure if it was an actual voice or if he was somehow imagining it.

"Yes!" Billos said. He might have spoken; he might have shouted—he didn't know. He only knew that his whole body screamed it.

Billos looked around. "Elyon?"

Why do you doubt me, Billos?

In that single moment the full weight of Billos's foolishness crashed in on him like a sledgehammer. He curled into a fetal position within the bowels of the lake and began to moan.

I see you, Billos.

I made you.

I love you.

The words washed over him, reaching into the deepest folds of his flesh, caressing each hidden synapse, flowing through every vein, as though he had been given a transfusion.

The water around his feet began to boil, and he felt the lake suck him deeper. He gasped, pulled by a powerful current. And then he was flipped over and pushed headfirst by the same current.

A dark tunnel opened directly ahead of him, like the eye of a whirlpool. He rushed into it, and the light fell away.

Pain hit him like a battering ram, and he gasped for breath. He instinctively arched his back in blind panic and reached back toward the entrance of the tunnel, straining to see it, but it had closed.

He began to scream, flailing in the water, rushing deeper into the dark tunnel. Pain raged through his body. He felt as if his flesh had been neatly filleted and packed with salt, each organ stuffed with burning coals, his bones drilled open and filled with molten lead.

Black's raspy chuckle filled his ears. Then his own laughter, as sinister as Black's, and he knew then that he had entered his own soul.

Billos involuntarily arched his back so that his head neared his heels. His spine stressed to the snapping point. He couldn't stop screaming. The tunnel gaped below him and spewed him out into soupy red water. Bloodred. He sucked at the red water, filling his spent lungs.

From deep in the lake, a moan began to fill his ears, replacing his own screams. Billos twisted, searching for the sound, but he found only thick, red blood. The moan gained volume and grew to a wail and then a scream of terrible pain.

Elyon was screaming.

Billos pressed his hands to his ears and began to scream with the other, thinking now that this was worse than the dark tunnel.

Then he was through. Out of the red, into the green of the lake, hands still pressed firmly against his ears. Billos heard the words as if they came from within his own mind.

I love you, Billos.

Immediately the pain was gone. Billos pulled his hands from his head and straightened. He floated, too stunned to respond.

I choose you.

Billos began to weep. The feeling was more intense than the pain that had racked him.

The current pulled at him again, tugging him up through the colors. His body again trembled with pleasure, and he hung limp as he sped through the water. He wanted to speak, to scream, to yell, and to tell the whole world that he was the most fortunate man in the universe. That he was loved by Elyon. Elyon himself.

Never leave me, Billos.

"Never! I will never leave you."

The current pushed him through the water and then above the surface not ten meters from the shore. He stood on the sandy bottom, retched a quart of water from his lungs, and straightened. For a moment he had such clarity of mind that he was sure he could understand the very fabric of space if he put his mind to it.

He was chosen.

And then a new thought mushroomed in his mind.

"Darsal."

When he spoke her name, light spilled from his lips and fell heavily to the water. He held up his hands and saw that light drifted off his fingertips. The boy's words came back.

I can give you something that makes his suhupow seem silly.

Run, Billos. Run.

Billos ran.

thirty-two

The dark stairwell swallowed Johnis and Silvie for the second time that night, or was it still day? Either way it hardly mattered. *We are plunging into eternal darkness,* Johnis thought.

"What are we doing?" Silvie's cry echoed down the stone enclosure, battering his ears. What? Exactly what, he didn't know.

"We have to get an advantage!"

"Down here?"

Johnis reached the bottom and rushed for the door that led into the tunnel.

"Johnis!"

He spun back, and as his body turned, the water bag in his right hand slipped out. It landed with a loud slap and, before Johnis could react, splashed its contents on the stone floor. A loud hissing and sizzling filled the atrium, then slowly faded.

"What did you do?"

"I have one more."

"We won't have enough to go back!" Silvie snapped. She couldn't hide the panic in her voice, and it only pushed Johnis closer to the same.

"You don't think I know?" he shouted, then shoved his hand into his last water bag. "How many bags do you have?"

"One more. This one's almost empty. Not enough, Johnis. We'll be stranded down here."

"And not above?"

"I'd rather die fighting than be stuck in a hole!" She strode back toward the stairs.

"No! Silvie, we can't go back up. It's death!"

"And this is not?" she shouted.

"Okay." He paced, trying to think. "Okay, calm down. We have water, right? We have the blessing of Elyon. We are on a noble mission."

"Noble warriors are the first to die," she pointed out.

And so they were. Johnis lowered his voice and spoke quickly. "Okay, forget the noble part. We have water. We go in, take Alucard hostage, threatening him with only one drop of water; that's all we need. We march him out, and he leads us from the forest."

"On foot? It'll take us a day."

"Better than a day down here."

"He knows that if we kill him, Billos or Darsal will die. They have a vow."

"We don't know that they will actually die! That could be fable."

"Like the Roush are fable? Like the Shataiki are fable? Do you want to take that chance?"

"No. But he can be made to think differently."

As if in answer, a loud thump echoed down the stairwell. The outer door closed.

Metal clanged.

And now the door was sealed.

"Great," Silvie said.

Johnis turned back to the door leading in and pulled it wide. "That settles it."

Silvie hesitated, then he heard her feet moving across the wet ground.

thirty-three

Darsal stood like a pole, refusing to look up at Karas. They'd hog-tied Karas the same way they'd tied Billos, then hoisted her up so that she hung like a bag of salt, belly down.

The girl was being brave, braver than anyone her age Darsal had met. Whether or not she really was her niece by blood, she was now a sister by a stronger bond. But even the bravest girl couldn't stop the tears that wet her pink cheeks.

Darsal had come expecting to give herself for Billos, only after convincing Karas to wait in the eatery with the books in the event she could set Billos free and would need a fast escape. But after agreeing, Karas had caught up to her at the edge of the temple and had offered a newly formed reason.

"Black wants the books," Karas had explained.

"So then get back there and guard them! Get out of here!"

"He'll take you in exchange for Billos, but you won't give him the books. So he'll kill you."

"You don't know that."

"I do, Sister. You're too principled to give him the books."

"Either way, there's nothing you can do. Now, get back!"

"I can't go back knowing that you'll die."

She had heard Billos crying out. They were running out of time!

"Please, I can't bear this!" Darsal had said. "Get back before I knock you out and drag you back."

"Then Billos will die," Karas had said. "My mind is set."

Billos had cried out again.

"Then you're a fool," Darsal had said. She had turned her back and was striding toward the temple, furious. But Karas had followed.

Now she hung like a hog to be slaughtered if Darsal didn't tell him where the books were. She had no choice. Say what she may, the young girl had grown on her.

"Okay!" Darsal snapped. "Let her down!"

"Where are the books?" Black asked.

"I'll show you."

The Dark One hesitated only a moment. He nodded at Claude.

"You sure? They killed Steve. We're owed."

Then the one named Black did something Darsal could never have predicted. His jaw snapped wide, twice as wide as she imagined possible, so that his chin slammed into his chest. Baring perfectly formed white teeth, he jerked his head forward and roared at Claude, who shrank back.

The man's jaw clacked shut. He stepped forward and lowered Karas.

"Show me," Black said.

Karas looked up at Darsal with round, apologetic eyes. Darsal marched forward, through the mob, around the corner. She scanned the village for a sign of Billos, but the weak-minded fool was nowhere to be seen.

According to Billos, Black needed them to find these books. Why, Darsal wasn't sure, but it gave her one final opportunity, however slim, to escape.

Then again, if Black kept her separated from the books, all hope was lost.

"I'm sorry, Sis," Karas said.

"Don't be."

"Keep your drums shut," Black said. "You can kiss and make up later."

Darsal led them to Smither's Barbeque and pushed the door open.

"That's far enough." The Dark One stepped past her, sauntered up to the bar, and turned around, wearing a sly grin. "Now. Come in, and keep your hands where I can see them."

She walked in, followed by Karas. Claude filled the doorway, long gun in hand. The rest stayed in the street, watching.

"Where are they?"

"You expect me to just give them to you?"

Black lifted his hand, and she watched it fill with a long gun with two barrels, stretched out toward Karas. "You expect me not to blow your little doll here all over the wall?"

He'd made his point. "How do I know you won't anyway?" she demanded.

"I'm going to count to three. One, two, thr—"

"Behind the counter."

"Get them out."

Black kept the gun on Karas, who stood too far away for Darsal to touch, no matter how well things went. And she wasn't going to leave the girl.

"Give me your assurance that you'll let us go if I give you these four, and I'll help you find the other three," she said.

"The other three? What makes you think I need your help?"

"Billos said you needed his help."

"To bring the four books to me from wherever they came. The rest was just to get his attention." The man smiled. "And for the record, the other three books aren't here. They're in the real world of Paradise. This"—he scanned the ceiling and walls—"is all a simulation of sorts. Real enough, but no flesh and blood. You're strapped in a chair at the moment, playing a game. The only way to enter the flesh-and-blood Paradise is through an open book. Unfortunately, once you do that, there's no going back. Ever."

What he was suggesting was nothing but a trick, of course. "If none of what I see is real, then neither are the books," she said. "They're useless."

"No, the books are outside all this. They're the only thing that *is* real here. Except me and your mind, that is. Which is why if I kill little Miss Muffet here, she dies. So it might as well all be real, *comprende?*"

She didn't *comprende*, whatever that meant.

"The books, if you would be so kind. Let's go on three again, shall we? One, two . . ."

The rear door crashed open. "Three."

Boom!

Darsal's breath caught in her throat. Billos appeared in the doorway and finished Black's threat. But the word hadn't left Billos's mouth before Black swiveled his gun and fired from both barrels.

A blast of heat swallowed her, from Billos's or Black's gun she wasn't sure at first. Light had blasted from Billos with that word, and it met the suhupow from the Dark One's gun head-on.

The light from Billos slammed into her, threatening to tear her clothes off. It rushed past her and smashed the glass from the eatery's windows like ten thousand fists.

Black stood in the face of the light for one moment, then grabbed his coat with one hand and turned into it. He spun and was gone. His last words echoed in the space he'd vacated.

"See you on the other side," he said.

The light collapsed back on Billos and winked out.

Darsal stared around, dumbfounded. The doorway where

Claude had stood was empty, as was the street beyond, she saw. Smither's Barbeque was gutted from inside out.

The light had simply and completely destroyed the darkness.

Billos stepped in, dripping wet, and stared at them.

"Well then," Karas said.

Somehow Darsal was certain that all this power would be gone when they returned to Middle Forest. The real question was whether Billos had truly changed.

A wry grin nudged his mouth. "Now, that's what I call power, baby."

Darsal strode to the counter, withdrew the four books, and plopped them on a table next to Billos—the only one left upright that she could see.

"Good to see you too," she said, looking up at Billos, who watched her with wide eyes, perhaps harboring remorse. Something had changed him, but that didn't mean she didn't have cause to be terrified by his behavior.

For the first time since entering the layer of reality that Black had insisted wasn't flesh and blood, Darsal remembered her sworn oath to Alucard. Perhaps she would soon have cause to be terrified by her behavior as well. They could probably leave this place by touching the books with blood, but then what? She didn't know.

The books were his by oath. Either the books or one of their lives.

"Let's get out of here," Billos said.

thirty-four

The library was empty.

Johnis and Silvie had rushed down the worm-infested tunnel and spun into Alucard's library, armed to the elbows with water, only to find the room vacated.

Silvie voiced the obvious. "He's gone."

Alucard was gone, but no fewer than a dozen shiny, thick worms slid along the walls of his lair now. The bookcase was wet with their mucus and the wall lumpy with their thick pink lengths. Johnis studied the leather-bound books in the case, ancient volumes that looked as though they hadn't been moved in a long time.

The flame on the wall spewed an oily smoke, crackling as it tongued at its own fumes. The only other sound was the soft clicking of worms sliding through their own paste in the tunnel behind them.

It occurred to Johnis that his thinking seemed to have slowed. He wondered if it had something to do with the air he and Silvie had subjected themselves to down here.

Silvie inhaled sharply, and Johnis followed her line of vision to a huge lump high on their right.

Alucard hung upside down by his feet from the corner ceiling. He was watching them with red glass globes, and his tongue was flickering at moist lips. Other than that he hung perfectly still, like a large cluster of rotten grapes.

Coiled around the beast's torso nestled a long, thick worm. Alucard's tongue reached for the mucus on the wall next to the worm, licked up a healthy portion, and withdrew the salve into his mouth.

All the while, not a word from the Shataiki. He seemed too distracted by his feeding or too smug in his confidence to react to their reappearance in his lair, which could only mean that his claim regarding Darsal's oath was indeed true.

"You've come back to kill me?" Alucard spoke around the slimy mucus in his throat, offering each word with delicacy. He followed his question with a long, low chuckle.

Silvie backed toward the desk opposite the hanging beast.

"Would you like some worm smack?" he asked, flicking his tongue out like a snake. "The blood of evil isn't red down here. Maybe if you drink, I'll give you safe passage out of my forest."

"So that we could return to burn it?"

"Burn it; I don't care anymore. This world is too restricting for me."

"And you think the world Billos and Darsal vanished to is waiting with open arms? You're condemned to hell, no matter where you go."

"I'm not interested in going where they went."

"Then what?"

Alucard closed his eyes and licked the mucus to his right with a long, slow, probing tongue. His mangy fur shivered with pleasure; a wet popping sound accompanied his swallowing.

His eyes opened red again, but he didn't answer.

"Kill him," Silvie whispered bitterly.

Johnis nearly flung the full contents of his bag at the Shataiki, knowing that something very evil had hatched behind those eyes. But there was more at stake here than Alucard's plotting.

"Darsal," he said.

"She made her choice. Our only way out is to cut the head off of this forest's power and get out while—"

"No. We can't leave without the books."

"You can't leave," Alucard said quietly from his corner. "With *or* without the books."

Johnis spun back, grabbed the gate, and slammed it shut. He shoved a bolt through the latch, effectively locking them in. "Our fate is yours," he said.

The bat chuckled. "I have all the food I need to live for a year

TED DEKKER

down here. What did you have in mind?" He licked at the wall again. "It's quite delicious . . . once you get used to it."

Silvie spat to one side.

"Your water is useless now," Alucard said. "You'll see that. I promissssss."

"We have no choice!" Silvie whispered, but her voice carried all too well in the stone chamber. "He's bluffing about the vow! We have to take our chances now!"

Johnis rubbed his submerged fingers together, considering. But his mind wasn't working as quickly as it had only minutes ago. His vision shifted, showing doubles, and he blinked to clear his head.

"Maybe . . ."

Alucard was suddenly a blur, launching himself from his corner faster than Johnis could have imagined. Unless he *was* imagining it.

One moment the Shataiki hung dumb; the next he was behind Johnis with a single talon hooked around his neck, ready to slice his jugular.

"Am I a fool?" the Shataiki hissed.

A dozen options slogged through Johnis's mind. None of them were immediately useful. The creature was right: their water would only keep them alive so long. They were doomed here in this lair. The only thing they could hope for was to take this prince of darkness with them.

"And the books?" Johnis asked.

256

Silvie seemed to understand. "We'll have to leave the mission to Darsal and Billos," she said. Then she reached out and touched his hand. Her voice trembled when she spoke. "I love you, Johnis."

He glanced at her misted eyes. But he saw something behind her that made him start. Peering through the gate was a sea of red eyes. Not normal Shataiki, but larger beasts, like Alucard. A dozen were on each side of an even larger beast, who drilled Johnis with a glare that seemed to reach into his eyes, down his spine, and to his knees, which began to shake.

Teeleh.

Silvie saw his look and spun around. The sight of so many larger Shataiki staring with such purpose changed everything in Johnis's mind. It was as if the beasts had expected this. Or at the very least, they were taking advantage of a situation they knew could only end well for them.

"Kill me, and there are a thousand who would take my place," Alucard said.

"Kill him!" Silvie screamed, and flung a fistful of water directly at Teeleh.

The water hit his chest and sizzled. A few drops splashed onto the bat to his right; he began to tremble.

Johnis learned two things then: The first was that these Shataiki didn't die as easily as the smaller variety. The second was that Teeleh was hardly affected at all.

His mangy coat smoldered and quivered but otherwise showed no indication he'd been attacked. His eyes held steady, slicing through Johnis like bloodthirsty daggers. The Shataiki next to him was now shaking badly. *It can be killed with the water*, Johnis thought. But he didn't know how much it would take.

All the while Johnis remained still. The talon at his neck suddenly lifted from his skin, and Alucard stepped back.

"Clearer now?"

They had enough water to kill Alucard, and perhaps the bat had feared for his life to that extent. But even if they used all the water they had with them, they could never escape the lair.

Silvie was still staring at Teeleh with a mixture of disbelief and horror. The beast did not move, did not speak, did not breathe, as far as Johnis could see. It was as if he'd come only to observe and give his blessing. To what end, Johnis could not know. But he knew now that there was no good ending to this misguided journey. They'd survived once, but they would not survive twice.

"What do you want?" he asked.

Johnis?

The voice that spoke in his mind belonged to little Karas, whom he'd rescued. All in vain. She was now haunting him.

Johnis!

He turned to his left, from the direction the voice came from in his mind. In his mind's eye Karas stood, holding the four Books of History, each wrapped in red twine. She was staring with wide eyes past him at Alucard, clutching her treasure in both hands. And on either side of Karas stood Darsal and Billos, scanning the room with darting eyes.

Johnis blinked away the vision. But the sight of Karas, Darsal, and Billos remained stubbornly unchanged. Karas looked at him again. "What's . . . what's happening?"

They were real. Here. All of them. With the books.

And this is why Teeleh is here, Johnis realized. *For the books.*

thirty-five

D o your bidding," Teeleh said.

Alucard stepped around Johnis and slowly approached the trio, who stood unmoved. His wings dragged behind as he slogged forward, but Johnis knew better than to be fooled by the sluggishness of his movements.

He stopped when he was halfway to Darsal, so that they formed a triangle with Alucard at one point, Johnis and Silvie at another, and their comrades at the third.

"Give me the books," he said.

"Not exactly what I had in mind," Billos said, looking at the worms on the wall. "I think I prefer the white room with DELL."

"This isn't good," Darsal said, her eyes fixed on Alucard.

"You made a vow," the beast said.

Darsal just stared, but Johnis knew she had. They would now find out what that meant.

"You can't, Karas," he said.

"Then give me her." Alucard stretched one talon toward Darsal.

"No." The muscles in Billos's jaw bunched. "Over my dead body."

"Perhaps. But the vow was made over the books. You can't use the books to undermine that vow. They cannot help you escape me, to whom you owe your life."

The words hung between them like knives that would slash flesh before this engagement was over. The only question was, whose flesh?

Teeleh and his entourage breathed and peered from their right, undisturbed. Unflinching. Unchallenged.

Johnis looked at Darsal. The water in his fist was now nearly useless. He could slow Alucard, but to what end?

"Darsal, tell us he's lying," Silvie said.

She swallowed and shifted on her feet. "There has to be a way out," she said.

Karas gripped the books tighter. "The books—"

"Are mine!" Alucard finished.

"That wasn't the oath!" Darsal said. She'd snapped out of her indecision and glared at the beast. "The books or me, that was the deal, and you, too, are bound by that oath! Otherwise you'd have taken them already."

Her eyes switched to Johnis, and she spoke urgently. "Touch the leather skin on the books with blood and you enter a simulation between this world and another. Open these four and you enter another reality entirely. The other three books are hidden there, Johnis, sought by the Dark One."

"The Dark One?" Johnis glanced at Teeleh, who hadn't removed his stare. The beast knew all of this already.

"Marsuvees Black," Billos said. "The magic man."

It made Johnis's head spin, this business of realities. But in many ways it was like being able to see the Roush and the Black Forest here, while most of the world remained blind to them.

Beyond the skin of these books waited another reality, bristling with power.

Darsal stared at Alucard. Bitterness laced her voice. "So take your spoils!" she said, spreading out her arms. "But the books belong to them!"

"What are you saying?" Billos cried. "Not on your life. No, not a chance!"

Alucard's eyes settled on the books in Karas's arms. "Then you offer yourself in her place?" he asked Billos.

"No, he doesn't," Darsal said. "No, Billos, you aren't! That wasn't the vow I made."

"Actually, it was," Alucard said. "Either one of you. Dead."

"Stop it!" Karas cried. "Stop arguing about who will die! We don't know that he isn't lying!"

Her voiced echoed, then the room settled into silence except

263

for the breathing that came from the Shataiki beyond the gate. Watching, ever watching.

"Then put it to the test," Alucard said.

"How?"

"Billos, do you accept the debt owed to me by Darsal?"

Darsal started to protest. "No, he—"

"Yes," Billos said.

"I accept your obligation," Alucard said. "You are now bound by the laws of the books and may not use them until you have paid your debt."

"Meaning what?" Darsal demanded, stepping forward.

"Meaning he can't use the books as long as he's alive. Unless, of course, you give me the books first."

"But . . ." She stared at Billos, then back at Alucard, lost for words.

"Show her, Billos. Open a book and see what happens."

Johnis jerked his hand from the bag and held it out without thinking of the water now dribbling to the floor. "No!"

The water hit the ground and sizzled. He'd nearly forgotten the power at his fingertips. But it wasn't enough now.

"No," he repeated. "We can't just open a book—"

"It's the only way out of here," Karas said.

She spoke the truth, and the Shataiki all seemed to know it. Then why were they standing by?

"Open the book, Billos."

He searched Darsal's eyes. They both knew that the books

might be Billos's only way to survive. If there was no way out through the books, he would be trapped here to face whatever fate the Shataiki found suitable.

"Open it," Darsal said in a thin voice.

Billos hesitated only one more moment, then reached for the green book on the stack of four in Karas's hands.

"The books have to be together to create the breach," Alucard said through dripping saliva, as if tasting a delicious fruit he'd waited his whole life to sink his teeth into. "Then the breach is accessed by any of the books until all four are gone. To return, a new breach must be created, using all four."

The breach he was talking about wasn't the same as the one that Billos had gone through. This gate opened by all four books would take them to a different place altogether: Earth.

"Are you sure this is a good idea?" Silvie asked.

Billos withdrew his knife and placed the blade on the string that bound the book. He looked at Johnis, who nodded.

The twine popped under the blade's sharp edge. Alucard held his ground. The room stilled.

"Open it," the beast said. His lips trembled with anticipation.

Billos rested one finger along the cover's edge, then lifted it open. Parchment browned with age faced them all.

But no magic. Nothing that indicated great power lay within. Not even words of another reality.

"Cut your hand. It needs blood."

Billos sliced his palm. Blood seeped from the wound.

"Put your hand on the page," Alucard said.

Billos's hand hovered above, then lowered to the open page. He let it rest there for a moment, then lifted his eyes.

"Nothing."

A coy smile twisted Alucard's lips. "You see?"

"Silvie," Johnis said. "Put your hand on the book."

"Yes, Silvie," Alucard said. "Enter the book."

Silvie glanced at the gate, then looked into Johnis's eyes. "If something happens—if I go somewhere—you'll come. Promise me."

"I promise."

She handed her water bag to Johnis, walked up to the book, cut her own palm, and unceremoniously placed her bleeding hand on the same page Billos had tried.

Only this time something did happen. This time the space where Silvie stood was suddenly spinning, as if she had become a funnel of dust, swirling in color, fading fast.

Johnis stood rooted, shocked at the sight of her transformation. The book began to suck her in.

"Do your bidding," Teeleh breathed behind them.

If Johnis had not been holding two bags, he might have been able to slow Alucard enough to prevent what happened next. The Shataiki streaked to the books with the same speed he'd shown earlier, slicing his palm with a talon as he moved.

Silvie vanished into the book just ahead of him, but Alucard reached them before Johnis could move, and he dove into the swirl that had swallowed Silvie.

The green book disappeared in a small flash of light.

Silvie and Alucard were both gone.

The sound of breathing behind the gate thickened. For a long moment no one in the room moved. The ramifications of what they'd just witnessed seeped in.

One, the books worked.

Two, a way of escape had been opened to them.

Three, where that escape would lead them was completely uncertain.

Four, Alucard had succeeded in his objective.

Five, Billos might as well be dead.

Talons grated on the gate. Johnis jerked around to see that two of the large Shataiki were opening the latch.

"Go!" he screamed, rushing forward.

"Billos?" Darsal reached for the man she loved.

Billos stepped up to Johnis, snatched both bags of water from his hands, whirled to Darsal, and kissed her on the lips.

When he pulled back, his eyes were fiery with determination. "Go!"

"Billos?"

"Go, Darsal. Never forget me."

"No!" She barged forward, grabbed one of the bags from his hands, and faced the coming Shataiki. She flung some water at them and they recoiled, smoldering. But the only cry was hers.

"I stay with you!"

"Darsal, no! Take her, Johnis!"

Johnis snatched one of the books from Karas and shoved it into Darsal's belt. "Use it!" he snapped, then turned back to Karas.

Working quickly, he popped the twine and threw the cover open as Karas did the same to the book in her hands. He sliced his palm, then hers when she hesitated.

"Ready?"

She glanced up at him with wide eyes, then Johnis shoved his palm flat on his book.

The world spun and then vanished. Johnis clenched his eyes tight, aware that he was suspended, but only for a moment before his feet felt solid ground.

Light exploded through the red in his eyelids. When he opened them again, he was standing in a desert. He blinked against a sun that hung overhead, white, blazing hot.

He was in a desert, but also on a plateau, overlooking a massive valley filled with a gray haze. Spread in the valley below was what looked to be a forest of sorts. Leafless trees of assorted shapes and sizes reached for the sky. Square, triangular, cylindrical . . .

No, not trees. This was a city. One that dwarfed the Horde city.

"Johnis?" a voice asked.

Johnis turned slowly and stared at Silvie, who was looking at him with wide eyes. She rushed up and threw her arms around his neck, rushing her words. "I was so worried . . . What took you so long? . . . I've been here for hours . . . I thought I'd been stranded!"

"Hours? It was less than a minute."

"No, no." She kissed him on the mouth. "Thank Elyon you're safe. I was sure I'd been sent to hell all alone."

Her whole body trembled against him, like a quivering puppy in his arms. He'd never seen her so upset. She pulled back, her eyes filled with tears. "I'm so afraid, Johnis. I don't know what's wrong with me."

"Shhh . . ." He kissed her forehead. "I'm here now. It's going to be okay." He glanced at the rise to their left.

Silvie followed his gaze. "I found a large placard over the hill. Big letters announcing a place named Las Vegas. But I couldn't bring myself to go any farther."

Silvie looked back into his eyes, then glanced about.

"Where are Karas and Darsal?"

thirty-six

Darsal knew the ending of their predicament already, and she accepted it with surprising calm. They would both die in the bowels of the Black Forest. But at least she wouldn't have to live without Billos. After all she'd been through to win him back, she wasn't going to leave him, never again.

Johnis had vanished, and then a few moments later Karas as well, leaving Billos and Darsal with the last book tucked in her waist.

"Back!" Billos cried, shoving her behind him as he flung a great handful of the water toward the gates.

Teeleh had vanished during the commotion, leaving only his henchmen to attend to his interests. Two of them lay writhing, claws clacking on the stones, but otherwise silent. No screaming from this bunch. They'd evolved beyond the common shrieks of lesser Shataiki.

The gate flew wide and filled with a red-eyed beast clearly intent on reaching them. Darsal stepped up and flung the entire contents of her bag on the fellow. The Shataiki stood still, skin smoldering and melting in parts. He slowly backed out, shaking head to foot.

Billos sprang forward, slammed the gate shut, and threw the bolt home. He flicked more water on the gathered Shataiki, then even more, pushing them away.

He jumped back, face red. "You have to leave, Darsal. You know you have to leave! Now, before the water's gone. It's just a matter of time."

His words cut like knives. "I can't, Billos." Tears blurred her vision. "I won't leave you again! Not now."

She felt her back hit the wall. Wet mucus from the worms seeped past her tunic, but she didn't care.

Billos pressed in close. He glanced to see that the Shataiki were closing in on the gate again, then set his bag down and faced her. There was no way to lock the gate properly—the beasts would be in soon enough to face another round of water until it was gone. And then they would have their way.

Billos took her hands in his. "Listen to me, Darsal."

"No, I can't. I won't; you can't ask this of me!"

He grabbed her face firmly, then softened his grip. "Listen to me."

His eyes bore into hers, and for a moment she lost herself in the stare of the man who'd saved her as a child and protected her a thousand times since. This man whom she loved more than she loved her own flesh.

They could say that Billos had abandoned them for his own gain. They could say that he thought of no one but himself. That he was a bull among clay pots. More muscle than heart, more passion than brains, more sword than sense.

He would as soon kill a woman as kiss one, they could say. As soon beat her in a race as marry her.

But Darsal knew the real man bearing down on her now. This was Billos, the mad, passionate adventurer who made her laugh in times of peace and rage in times of battle. He'd given her life, and she'd made him the man he was today, faults and all.

Indeed, it was the fact that he was flawed that made her, a deeply flawed woman herself, so comfortable with him.

"You are my life, Darsal." His voice was soft but urgent. "I made my choice to—"

"You had no right," she cried.

He took a breath and started again. "I made my choice days ago, weeks ago, years ago. Those choices ended today in the lake I told you about, remember?"

He'd told her before they'd touched the books with blood in Paradise. Whatever happened there had been the stuff of mind-bending reality, whether they were seated in chairs hooked up to DELL or not. It was as real as any of this.

Billos had been changed in Elyon's lake.

"The lake gave you life! How dare you consider death now!"

Claws clacked on the gates. The bolt slid slowly back. The Shataiki were wary, but coming.

"Because this part of my life is over. There is no more for me. Except you." Billos touched her face gently, traced the scar on her cheek. He leaned forward and touched his lips to hers.

Darsal felt as though a sledgehammer was trying to force its way up her throat. Her shoulders shook in silent sobs.

He spoke through the gentle kiss. "I love you, Darsal." His breath was hot on her mouth. Musky and sweet. She longed to taste it the rest of her life. "Live so that I can die knowing I've saved you. Please, I beg you, I beg—"

"No!" Darsal cried, placing her hands on his chest and shoving him away. Then leaning into a scream, "No!"

She grabbed the water bag from him, marched up to the gate, and sent the Shataiki reeling with a huge splash. She slammed the gate, shoved the bolt down, and spun back.

"You can't do this to me . . ." But her voice faltered. Then she couldn't speak for the fist in her throat. She stood limp, shaking with terrible sobs. Darsal felt his arms pull her in, and she fell into his chest willingly. For a long moment he just held her, drawing his fingers along her back as she wept into his neck.

Behind her the gate began to rattle again. The Shataiki were coming, and this time there wasn't enough water to push them back.

The book pressed into her waist where Johnis had shoved it.

Billos spoke frantically. "You have to tell Johnis everything! The white room and Paradise were only a reflection of reality, like a game. A skin or a book's cover. But the real Paradise exists. On Earth. Marsuvees Black is the Dark One. Three of the books are hidden on Earth, but with these four all seven will be on Earth and will be visible to anyone. You have to tell Johnis."

The bolt was sliding.

"He knows! It's not a reason—"

"*I'm* the reason!" Billos shouted. Then he spoke softer, his eyes reaching beyond her to the gate. "Live for me. We'll open the book and touch it together. If I am meant to go with you, I will."

She didn't feel like she could move. The gate squealed. Billos grabbed the book from her waistband, popped the red twine, and flipped it open before her.

"For me," he said.

Darsal looked into his eyes. He was asking her to do this for him. It was the last thing she would ever do for him. But she loved him too much to deny him this one dying request.

She leaned forward and kissed him hard. Then pulled back and set her jaw. "I love you desperately, Billos of Southern. You are my chosen one."

A grin tugged gently at his right cheek. "I am, huh?"

He winked. Then he shoved his hand on the opened page.

Two thoughts crowded Darsal's mind. The first was that the Shataiki were breathing down her neck. The second was that Billos wasn't disappearing.

He suddenly grabbed her hand, sliced it open, and flattened it against the page. "And now I choose you."

Darsal made another vow then, her hand on the book. *I will avenge your death, Billos. I will wage war on all who caused you to die until the day of my own death.*

Then her world spun and blinked to black.

thirty-seven

Johnis and Silvie stood on the cliff, silenced by the sheer size of the hazy valley before them.

A sea of towering buildings, gray from this distance, had been built between ribbons of flat rock that crawled with horseless buggies. Whole structures looked to be as large as all of Middle under one roof. The city below would make the Horde city seem a village by comparison.

"What do you think?" Silvie asked, voice tight.

"I think I prefer the Horde."

Silvie looked at the two Books of History under his arm. "This was a mistake. We're down to two books. We don't even know if Karas and Darsal made it through. How are we supposed to find all seven books in this place cursed by Elyon?"

"You think Alucard is here?"

She didn't respond. Her hand took his and tightened. Not out of affection, he knew, but because she knew more terror now than she ever had and needed a hand of comfort. Johnis knew this because he, too, felt . . . fear. More fear than was reasonable.

"We made the right choice, Silvie." But even as he said it, doubt skipped through his mind. "We're here to find the seven books before the Dark One does. We'll do that or die trying."

"Spoken like the good old Johnis we all know so well." She said it with a bite of frustration.

"Something's wrong with us," he said. "I don't feel myself."

"Really? You just now noticed?"

He returned his attention to the valley. A dull roar rose from the city. "So . . . where are we?"

"I told you," Silvie said. "We're in hell."

the end

THE BOOKS OF

CIRCLE TRILOGY

CIRCLE GRAPHIC NOVELS

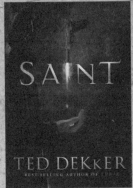

AN EXCERPT FROM

TED DEKKER'S NEXT NOVEL . . .

$INNER

COMING SEPTEMBER 2008

CHAPTER ZERO

MARSUVEES BLACK reread the words penned on the yellow sheet of paper, intrigued by the knowledge contained in them. He felt exposed, almost naked against this sheet of pulp that had come his way.

August 21, 2033

Dear Johnny –

If you're reading this letter, then my attempt to help you has failed and I've gone to meet my Maker. I don't have much time so I will be brief. None of what's happened to you has been by accident, Johnny—I've always known this, but never with as much clarity as now, after being approached by a woman named Karas who spoke of the Books of Histories with more understanding than I can express here.
Where to start . . .

The world is rushing to the brink of an abyss destined to swallow it whole. Conflict between the United States, Israel and Iran is escalating at a frightening pace. Europe's repressing our economy. Famine is over-running Russia, China's rattling its sabers, South America is battling the clobbering disease—all terrible issues, and I could go on.

But these challenges pale in comparison to the damage that pervasive agnosticism will cause us. The disparaging of ultimate truth is a disease worse by far than the Raison Strain.

Listen to me carefully, Johnny. I now believe that all of this was foreseen. That the Books of Histories came into our world for this day.

As you know, the world changed thirteen years ago when Project Showdown was shut down. Myself and a dozen trusted priests sequestered thirty-six orphans in the monastery in an attempt to raise children who were pure in heart, worthy of the ancient books hidden in the dungeons beneath the monastery. The Books of Histories, which came to us from another reality, contained the power to make words flesh. Whatever was written on their blank pages became flesh. If the world only knew what was happening!

Billy used the books to write raw evil into existence in the form of Marsuvees Black. A living, breathing man who now walks this earth, personifying Lucifer himself. He (and I cringe at calling Black anything so humane as a "he") was defeated once, but he hasn't rested since that day. There are others like him, you know that by now. At least four maybe many more, written by Black himself from several pages he managed to escape with. I believe he's used up the pages but he's set into motion something that he believes will undo his defeat. Something far more ominous than killers who come to steal and destroy in the dead of night. An insidious evil that walks by day, shaking our hands and offering a comforting smile before ripping our hearts out.

Billy may have repented, but his childish indiscretions will plague the world yet, as much as Adam's indiscretion has plagued the world since the garden.

Yet all of this was foreseen! In fact, I am convinced that all of these events may have been allowed as part of a larger plan. The Books of Histories may have spawned raw evil in the form of Black, but those same books also brought forward truth. And with that truth, your gifting. Your power!

And Billy's power. And Darcy's power. (Though they may not know yet)

Do you hear me, son? The West may be overrun with a populace that teeters on the brink of disbelief while at the very same time being infested with the very object of their disbelief. With incarnate evil! Black and the other walking dead.

But there are three who stand in the way. Johnny, Billy, Darcy.

Black is determined to obtain the books again. If he does, God help us all. Even if he fails, he escaped Paradise with a few pages and can wreak enough havoc to plunge the world into darkness. I am convinced that only the three of you stand in his way.

Find Billy. Find Darcy. Stop Black.

And pray, Johnny. Pray for your own soul. Pray for the soul of our world.

David Abraham

Marsuvees frowned. *Yes, pray, Johnny. Pray, for your pathetic, wretched soul.*

He crushed the letter in his gloved hand, shoved it into the bucket of gasoline by his side, and ignited the thing on fire using a lighter he'd withdrawn from his pocket after the first reading. Flames whooshed high, enveloping his hand along with the paper.

He could have lit the fire another way, of course, but he'd learned a number of things from his experimentation these last years. How to blend in. Be human. Humans didn't start fires by snapping their fingers.

He'd learned that subtlety could be a far more effective weapon than some of the more blatant methods they tried.

Black dropped the flaming page to the earth and flipped his wrist to extinguish the flame roaring about his hand. He ground the smoldering ash into the dirt with a black, silver-tipped boot and inhaled long through his nostrils.

So, the old man had known a thing or two before dying, enough to unnerve a less informed man than Black. He already knew Johnny and company were the only living souls who stood a chance of slowing him down.

But he was taking care of that. Had taken care of that.

Marsuvees spit into the black ash at his feet. Johnny's receipt of this letter would have changed nothing. It was too late for change now.

And in the end there was faith, hope and love.

No . . . in the end there was Johnny, Billy, and Darcy. And the greatest of these was . . .

. . . as clueless as a brick.

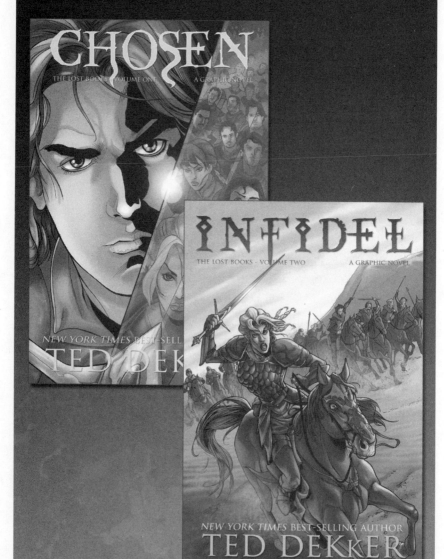

THE LOST BOOKS
THE MAKING OF THE GRAPHIC NOVELS

At Thomas Nelson we are passionate about storytelling and enjoy the thrill of introducing exciting new authors to readers for the first time. But we are equally passionate about surprising our best-selling authors' fans by retelling their favorite tales in fresh ways.

Joining us for a behind-the-scenes look at one way we are doing that is Kevin Kaiser, a writer and Editor in Chief of the Lost Books graphic novels, which are based on Ted Dekker's best-selling young adult novels.

Thomas Nelson: Thanks for joining us, Kevin. What exactly is a graphic novel?

Kevin Kaiser: It's really just a long-form comic book. Imagine taking your favorite novel and seeing the heroes, villains, and the world they occupy come to life visually. *That's* what a graphic novel is: an illustrated story. In a way, it's words becoming flesh.

TN: Describe the Lost Books graphic novels. How is the story different from the books?

KK: When storytelling is involved, it's tough to beat Dekker, so the story in the graphic novels unfolds as it does in the books. But we did wrap it in a slightly different skin. We adapted each book (about 260 pages) into four, 132-page comic books. Fans will notice immediately that the story is compressed, so the pacing is much faster—if you can imagine that with a Dekker story.

TN: What kind of quality would comic fans find if they picked up these books?

KK: Well done is better than well said, so I'll let these books speak for themselves. I will say this much: most of our production team has worked for DC Comics, Marvel and other top-tier publishers in the business. They aren't wannabe artists; they are world-class professionals. To see what I mean fans should pick up the Circle Trilogy graphic novels or visit **www.thecircletrilogy.com** to see some of their previous work.

TN: You mentioned the Circle Trilogy graphic novels, which you also produced. Tell us about the process. How does a novel become a graphic novel?

KK: It's a very involved process that takes about a year from concept to shelf. In many ways, adapting a novel into a visual format is similar to filmmaking. In fact, some of the most popular films in past years were graphic novels first. Let me walk you through the process.

CASTING CALL

KK: Several things happen at once, but we generally begin with concept art. First, we go through the book, make a descriptive profile for each character, and ask lots of questions. What color is this character's hair? How tall is he? What kind of clothes does he wear? We then work with the artists to flesh out (literally!) what each character should look like. It involves input from a team of people, including Ted himself, engaging in lively discussion.

Think about the last time you read a book. Did you have a fully formed image in your mind's eye of what a character looked like? You probably did, but maybe not as detailed as you think. Generality is not a luxury we have. Not only do we have to capture a character's appearance in detail, but also their personality and mannerisms. You only get one chance to design characters and the world they live in, so we want to get it right. Add on top of that several people who are involved in the process, and each of them has different ideas of what a character should and shouldn't be. It involves a lot of trial and error.

Below are two options for what Billos would look like. We ultimately chose the one on the left.

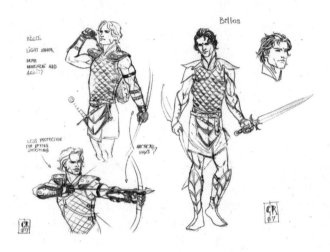

THE SCRIPT

KK: Next is writing the script. Just as every film needs a screenplay for the director and actors to follow, our artists need a script so they know how to draw a particular page.

The process begins with our writing team, led by the talented JS (Jeff) Earls, dividing each book into distinct "acts" and then outlining the book chapter by chapter, noting the main "beats" of the story. We then work through where the story can be streamlined, where it can't, and what story elements we could deliver in other ways. Remember, we only have 132 pages to tell the same story Ted told in 260, so brevity is essential. To give you context, that equals about 250 words per page in the novel, but only about 30-50 per graphic novel page.

Each graphic novel page is then written in screenplay format, then ruthlessly edited and rewritten until it's right. The end result is a "road map" of narrative (what's happening) and dialogue (what the characters are saying) to guide the artists in the next step.

Below is an example of a scripted scene from Chosen

CHOSEN, Page 9, Adapted by JS Earls

Panel 1 - Very dramatic two-shot of the Red team's Silvie (in front) and Jackov (close behind) running toward (us) the bouncing Horde Ball!

JACKOV
Grab the ball, Silvie. I'll take care of Billos.

SILVIE
I'm on it.

Panel 2 - Silhouette long shot of Silvie leaping high into the air (above the mound), reaching her arms out, her fingers almost touching the ball. On the ground, behind her - Jackov rushes forward. On the ground, in front of her - Billos approaches with Darsal close behind.

Panel 3 - Close-up of Silvie's hands grabbing the Horde Ball.

Panel 4 - Action shot of Silvie, hunched over (like a "cannonball"), cradling the ball in her gut as she rolls in the air. Below her, Billos reaches up for Silvie, but she is out of his reach.

SILVIE 2
Now, Jackov!

Panel 5 - Violent view of Jackov diving into Billos, tackling him hard enough to knock the wind out of Billos and lift his feet from the ground!

BILLOS (LOUD)
OoOof!

ROUGH LAYOUT

KK: Next up is layout, when the storytelling baton is passed from the writer/adapters to the artist. The lead artist takes the script and translates the written word into action for the first time. Like a cinematographer, his job is to breathe life into a scene through camera angles, perspective, and scene flow. Significant thought is invested into layouts, and we explore several combinations of panel size, type and arrangement until we find just the right look and feel for a page. Below is an artist's rendering of the script on the previous page.

You'll notice that the art is not very refined. That's intentional. A layout is just the artist's rough draft of a page, and it gives us the chance to tweak different elements of a scene quickly. That even includes ensuring there is room for the speech bubbles. Notice the numbered captions, which are tied to dialogue from the script. Only after we have settled on an overall feel that is right will the artist draw the final art.

FINAL ART AND INKS

KK: After the layout is finalized, the artist draws the page in detail. This is the first time the page begins to look like it will in the book, though it is certainly far from complete. After it is drawn, the page then goes through a rigorous editorial process to ensure the visual story is sharp. We look at *every* detail, including things like making sure a character's shadow falls in the right place given the angle of the lighting in the panel. Every detail is important. But again, it takes time. On average, each page takes a full working day to draw, not including any revisions that will need to be made during the editorial process.

Here is the next phase of the same scene depicted on the previous page

COLORING AND LETTERING

KK: After everything is drawn and finalized, everything goes to another team of artists who specialize in digital coloring. From there, each page then goes to a letterer who inserts all of the speech bubbles, sound effects and captions. And, you have a graphic novel. Of course, there's all of the post-production work, assembly, printing, and manufacturing left to be done. But, we'll save that conversation for another day. (Laughs.)

Scene with lettering and sound effects

TED DEKKER is known for novels that combine adrenaline-laced stories with unexpected plot twists, unforgettable characters, and incredible confrontations between good and evil. Ted lives in Austin with his wife LeeAnn and their four children.